THE
LEADING
INDICATORS

GREGG EASTERBROOK

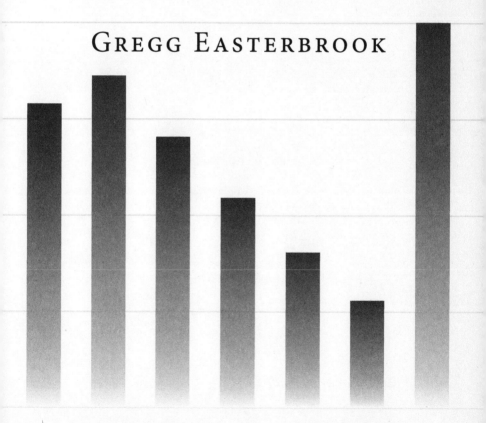

THOMAS DUNNE BOOKS 🌊 ST. MARTIN'S PRESS · NEW YORK

This is a work of fiction. All of the characters, organizations, and events portrayed in this novel are either products of the author's imagination or are used fictitiously.

THOMAS DUNNE BOOKS.
An imprint of St. Martin's Press.

THE LEADING INDICATORS. Copyright © 2012 by Gregg Easterbrook. All rights reserved. Printed in the United States of America. For information, address St. Martin's Press, 175 Fifth Avenue, New York, N.Y. 10010.

www.thomasdunnebooks.com
www.stmartins.com

Design by Steven Seighman

ISBN 978-1-250-01173-2 (hardcover)
ISBN 978-1-250-01174-9 (e-book)

First Edition: November 2012

10 9 8 7 6 5 4 3 2 1

To Michael Carlisle,

my literary agent

and my friend

The greatest crimes are caused by surfeit, not by want.

—Aristotle

THE
LEADING
INDICATORS

Chapter 1

October 2006

Dow Jones Index: 11,200.
Unemployment: 4.8 percent.
U.S. motor vehicle production: 11.2 million.

Even when they are what you expect, things still come as a surprise. The delivery driver should have known better than to feel blindsided when he hit a freeway traffic jam at six A.M. Carmine taillights in the still-dark meant thousands had left early to beat the backups. Not long before, a person needed to be out of the house by seven A.M. to reach work before the freeways clogged. Then by six-thirty, now by six—nobody need be reminded where that trend was headed. Vehicles descended toward the city with vehement determination, tiny parts inside their engines spinning too rapidly to see, men and women inside the cars alone gulping coffee and listening on the radio to agitated voices discussing an outrage or crisis or scandal. There seemed to be a lot of that going around.

The predawn traffic was beautiful in a way only our forebears could appreciate, since they could not have dreamed of society being able to build so many roads and place so many machines on them, while today it is hard to imagine these things not existing. No one planned or wanted the traffic jam, of course. A lot happens that isn't planned.

Coming over a rise, the driver hit the brakes as congestion worsened. There were lines of cars on the ramps, anxious to join the slowness. A bit farther along he exited and sought the convenience store where he always stopped—Grab 'N' Get Out, a popular chain, with a logo of a stylized giant mouth. The inside was busy, clerks in smocks dispensing ice-based drinks, breakfast tacos, candy bars, cigarettes, chili dogs and microwaved bacon sandwiches to customers in construction overalls, office attire, hospital scrubs, jogging suits. Within the realm of the modern American twenty-four-hour store, if the blinds were drawn it would become impossible to sense the time outside.

The driver chose a thirty-two-ounce Pepsi with a double vanilla shot and a jumbo popcorn, waiting to pay behind a man who, at 6:09 A.M., was purchasing a travel-sized laundry detergent and two lottery tickets. Headlines on morning newspapers stacked on a rack referred to developments in several wars, but the driver never talked with his friends about wars. They did talk a lot about combat video games. The driver hurried on his way to the distribution center, knowing he'd be docked an hour of pay if reporting more than three minutes late.

At the center, workers were nearing completion of the sorting of packages that arrived during the night. The sorting shift began at one A.M. Students from the local community college, welfare-to-work single moms and recent parolees dragged themselves in while most folks slept. They earned $11.50 an hour assigning to the proper truck routes the express packages, merchandise and documents borne to the city by cargo aircraft painted with bright insignia. Short-range planes began hitting the runways of a nearby airfield not long after midnight, depending on weather. Sorters had to work fast so a backlog didn't develop before the large long-distance cargo aircraft—heavies, to air controllers—arrived as the night was ending. Approaching, the cargo pilots sometimes saw the sunrise from high in the air, then descending to the ground, saw the sunrise a second time while taxiing.

A huge digital clock, electric numerals a foot high, hung on the wall by the distribution center entrance. More digital time readouts were stationed throughout the sorting area, arranged such that every worker had a clear view of a clock. The entry clock read 6:32 as the driver walked in.

"Just made it—I'll get you next time," said his supervisor, a strict woman who liked to penalize the drivers. She wore two cell phones, each in a hip holster like a gunfighter's six-shooters, plus a radio with earpiece as worn by a bodyguard or commando, and had a portable printer attached to her belt. She made jangling sounds when she moved.

The supervisor looked out into the parking lot at other delivery drivers who were parking their cars and couldn't possibly reach the entrance by 6:33 A.M., the cutoff time. There were several whom she would dock for being a mere moment late. This made her smile.

Bright lights inside the distribution center were nearly blinding: it was important the scanner devices had sufficient light to read bar codes accurately. The lights were the very latest low-energy models. The corporation liked to boast of environmental awareness, putting statistics about reduced carbon emissions at the top of press releases that mentioned outsourcing and canceled health benefits at the bottom.

Hourly laborers were moving boxes and sheen-material envelopes, timed on their average seconds per package handled. Not laborers—"associates," as if it were a communal undertaking. Computers did the thinking, directing what should go where.

Most of the products passing through the sorting center were designed or conceived in the United States or European Union, then made in Asia or Central America. Digital code representing a new video game, or a fashion touch just seen on a movie star, was beamed by Internet to fabrication facilities—they weren't factories anymore; no investor wants to hear the steam-era word "factory"—in the developing world, where workers assembled whatever struck the mood of the Western consumer at that instant. Jumbo jets guided by satellite navigation pulses picked up the goods that the developing world facilities produced. Sea transit was too slow: jets were required to ensure the orders arrived before a consumer mood swing. When dinnertime came the Asian workers sat at long tables for bowls of company-provided soup. At night they lived in dormitories so they could send their pay home to the village. The workers' cafeterias and dorms in Central America were guarded by teenagers with automatic weapons, nervous about dying in a shootout with a drug gang.

The delivery driver grabbed his day's assignment sheets. He took one of the new memory sticks to insert into his portable scanner, beginning his day's timings. Everything he did, down to bathroom breaks, would be timed.

The driver jogged, rather than walked, to his truck to help the preloaders prepare it by placing packages and envelopes into the reverse order they would be removed. The preloaders too ran back and forth, never merely walking. Once deliveries commenced, the driver would run from his truck to homes or offices, then run back. If delivering or picking up items that required dollies, he was allowed to walk when dragging a dolly that held weight, but expected to run when it was empty.

A generation previously, overnight nationwide delivery was not available even to the aristocratic. Now if a package containing a shirt or child's toy did not arrive at the correct door the next day for a nominal charge, people were irate. Accomplishing this was possible only if drivers ran from curb to stoop, if single moms reported to sorting centers in the middle of the night, if associates waived their lunch breaks. Still customers complained about the cost. Should the package contain a video game or new-model mobile phone, its price would not be possible unless big public companies pressured Asian suppliers to treat their labor force as glorified livestock. Still customers complained about the cost.

As the driver departed for his day's route, yellow sun was beginning to heat the city. Now the highways were packed with cars, trucks and buses. Developments such as cell phones and Web connections made aspects of life less time-consuming, but the time saved was mainly shifted to driving and thereby lost, netting no gain. Often not even shifted to driving, rather to sitting in barely moving cars. The backed-up roads were among the contemporary influences bringing out the worst in people. Men and women who were polite in person became, once in cars, Hun horsemen charging across the steppes. They would maneuver madly, horn blowing, to get a single car-length ahead, as if there were a reward for doing so. All that effort to attain the nice car, and the world refused to get out of your way.

Leaving the highway, the delivery driver beheld a

portion of the glowing suburban alternate universe that swells from the nation's cities. Homes, townhouses, offices, schools, stores, restaurants, filling stations, all with cars parked in every available spare bit of square footage, including, on the less pricey streets, on what were once lawns, now paved over to create parking space for the three- to five-car household, or for immigrant families squeezed in together. In much of suburbia, the car-to-adult ratio approaches 1:1. So many resources had been brought to bear to build suburbia and its automobile network that it was a wonder the Earth wasn't hollowed out and in danger of collapse. People might be struggling financially, but cars are doing really great.

Once off the highway, the driver retracted his truck's sliding doors and locked them in the open position, making his "package car," as the drivers called their vehicles, appear to have no doors. Except on the coldest days, express-delivery drivers keep the doors stowed, to save precious seconds. One hundred stops a day, one hundred openings and closings of a truck door—that's a lot of wasted time.

The driver ran, ran, ran through the morning part of his route, thinking about the World Series or about lunch. Arriving on Cobblestone Lane, where there were no sidewalks, much less cobblestones, he delivered North Face jackets and desktop printers. The neighborhood was the kind where the dimensions of a house served not just to contain what was within, but as an advertisement.

The truck approached the curved driveway of a regular, Margo Helot, to whom delivery companies brought packages nearly every day. The Helot household rested on a crest of tasteful affluence. Five-bedroom home fully redecorated. Two delightful children with good grades. His-and-hers fancy cars in the drive—Margo drove a Lexus, described by the automotive press as an "entry-level luxury" product. Day after day the driver brought this house packages from the kinds of places from which all Americans wished they were receiving packages: Williams-Sonoma, Bergdorf Goodman, Under Armour, Pfaelzer Brothers, L.L.Bean, Villeroy & Boch. Packages from L.L.Bean: a person could feel good about that, because this business is still independent and still makes its wares in Maine. At least, that's what they want you to believe.

Needing to pick up his pace, the driver swung his truck into the Helots' drive. Delivery personnel were supposed to stop on the street so as not to inconvenience a homeowner who might require the driveway at the same moment a package arrives. But drivers trying to shave time may take shortcuts.

The truck started up the curved incline toward the house. There was the sound of an enormous beer can being crushed. The driver's head jerked forward, then backward as the airbag fired. Behind his eyelids he saw the miniature lightning bolts depicted in cartoons when a talking raccoon is hit by a falling anvil.

The UPS and FedEx trucks, one arriving and moving forward, one departing and backing up too fast, had collided in the driveway.

Hearing the metallic crunch, Margo came to the door. Observing the collision, she ran to see if anyone was hurt. As she did this, a DHL truck pulled up. It takes a lot of deliveries to sustain a high-end lifestyle.

Chapter 2

Record North American heatwave ends.
Snow falls in Jerusalem.
Xbox 360 sales reach 10 million.
National debt: $7 trillion.

Margo Helot was easily dislodged by the small complications of life. The wide-screen television controller with its fifty-six buttons bearing cryptic labels like PIP/SWAP could make her lose it—fifty-six buttons, and just try turning the TV on. But Margo was composed at moments of distress. She ran to the injured driver, recognized arterial bleeding, applied pressure to stanch the blood. Margo had to twist her body sideways, squeezing against the driver, to get the correct angle to clamp his wound. She did not hesitate or waver, though she was splashed with quite a bit of blood and pressed hard against a strange man.

"Dial 911, then get the first-aid kit from the mud-room," she called to her friend Lillian Epperson, who was watching the scene in rapt horror, too frightened to move. Lillian was an academic and successful in her chosen field, but, well, you know about academics.

"The first-aid kit—go!" Margo's voice was commanding.

Margo had been a Gold Award Girl Scout, the equivalent of an Eagle Scout, and had done well in first-aid training. Why, she had then wondered, didn't the top girls receive a classy rank like Eagle—eagles are decisive animals—rather than a Gold Award, which sounds like a prize for best-dressed? When they moved into the house, Margo mounted the first-aid kit on the wall labeled with its bright green-and-white cross image so her daughters could find it quickly if something happened when she wasn't there. Not that Margo ever allowed them to be on their own.

Already there was the sound of a siren in the distance, the echo growing louder. The other driver, unhurt, was impressed that Margo knew what to do and was not afraid of blood.

"Got to—call my—supervisor—explain—delay," the injured driver said, groggy. Margo told him not to open his eyes, because of the blood.

"Shit, he's right, I better call in and report why I'm stopped," the other driver said, and bolted back to his truck. GPS tracking had just become practical, and companies were installing the devices in their vehicles. When a delivery truck stopped moving for more than a moment, the company wanted to know why. Unscheduled soda breaks or fifteen-minute naps were out of the question. If you needed a little time away from the monotony of delivering, you had to be driving—keep the truck in motion to satisfy the GPS. As long as fossil fuels were being consumed, it counted as work.

"Is he going to live?" Lillian asked. She was terrified the driver might die, and excited at the thought of being present at a death. Medical examiners, news helicopters—wait till her friends heard.

"He's going to have a monster headache, and the next time he goes out for drinks with the other drivers, he's going to make this crash sound a lot more dramatic than it was," Margo replied.

Lillian looked on, simultaneously frightened by the blood and trying to get a better view. She appeared to be expecting Margo to do something. But Margo could not remove her hands until the ambulance arrived—a clamped wound must remain clamped—and that meant Margo couldn't move.

"Maybe you should go inside," she told Lillian. Margo knew the EMTs would inject painkiller near the wound, then wrap the site for the ride to the hospital, and the driver would howl when a big needle went into a place that already hurt like hell. That was a moment Lillian should miss. Margo felt relief that the driver's gash did not contain any glass or metal, because she remembered that with arterial bleeding, the first responder should not try to remove any objects in the wound. Just apply pressure—no matter how much the victim screams.

The DHL driver walked up to Lillian nonchalantly and asked, "Can you sign for this?"

"Part for the espresso machine," Margo said of the package, a shade apologetically. "The espresso maker is as complicated as a steel foundry, but saves twenty minutes stopping at Starbucks."

Margo had to reposition her body to maintain firm pressure on the driver's wound. She was pressing hard against him: they were getting quite familiar.

The ambulance siren grew louder. "I did a time budget," Margo told Lillian. "I was stopping at the Starbucks four days a week, total of eighty minutes. Projected over the next ten years, that came to twenty-nine days—a whole month of my life would be spent in line at Starbucks while people were ordering shade-grown blueberry-almond drinks with names like Rapafrapazapachino. So I bought an espresso machine for the kitchen, twenty-five hundred dollars. Needs new parts pretty often. But added twenty-nine days to my life."

The DHL driver blanched at the thought of a $2,500 coffeemaker. He'd have to work two months to clear that amount, after taxes and child-support payments. Lillian signed for the package, and the DHL driver smiled and hustled back to his truck. The guy wanted to be moving again before emergency vehicles, turning down the street, pulled up and blocked his path. The delay would be bad for his electronic rating for the day. There was no way his dispatcher would buy some story about stopping to assist at a crash of competitors' trucks.

Lillian said, "Coffeemaker that costs more than a furnace—only in America!"

"Lillian, a new furnace is seven thousand dollars," Margo said.

"That much! I'd no idea what they cost. I've always lived in apartments." At this point Margo and Lillian were holding a genteel conversation though Margo was splashed with a fair amount of warm blood.

The ambulance arrived, turning into the street with

a cinematic screech. "Lillian, go inside!" Margo commanded.

To the emergency crew, accustomed to dealing with people who either just had horrible bad luck or just did something deeply stupid, the driveway crash seemed humdrum.

The EMTs worked quickly and efficiently. One took over applying pressure, allowing Margo to ease out of the truck's cab. Another prepared a gurney, a third brought the painkiller and bandages to stabilize the victim for transport.

Margo was splattered with blood, as if she were auditioning for a slasher film. "Thanks for getting here fast," she said. "He was starting to look a little cyanotic."

An EMT asked Margo if she was a doctor, and the compliment made her day. Then he advised her, "Strip immediately. Get into the shower and turn the water as hot as you can bear. Bleach your clothes on extended hot cycle. You know nothing about this guy."

There was something faintly titillating about being ordered to strip by a handsome stranger. A police car, a fire engine, a fire captain's car, then a second police car arrived to join the ambulance. There were numerous crackling radios, people in uniform reporting information in clipped codes. It seemed as though the military had come to occupy the street.

Neighbors stayed inside, watching from their windows, when the accident had just occurred and their help was needed. Now that the neighbors clearly were not needed, they came out to ask if there was anything they could do.

The ambulance departed with the driver: he was sitting up, his bleeding controlled, and smiling after a hypo of morphine. Margo completed paperwork for a policeman, who seemed shockingly young for a position of such authority. She stood in the driveway with fresh blood dripping down her breasts, casually talking to him.

The two women entered the house. "He had a *gun*," Lillian said, as though this were a news flash regarding a police officer. It occurred to Margo that her friend had never seen a real firearm. As instructed, Margo went directly to the shower, and fairly scorched herself.

Being inside lent a sensation of abundance. The many rooms, more than Margo's family of four needed, by their number testified to the ability to pay for such things. There was expensive furniture, paint chosen by a color consultant, the open-plan kitchen endorsed by architecture magazines. And perfect cleanliness.

Margo had the house cleaned twice a week, paying the Guatemalan woman fifteen dollars an hour. Some of her well-to-do neighbors paid half that and shouted over the slightest error, knowing the cleaning women were illegals who would never dare talk back. Margo wrote down the names of her cleaning woman's children and always asked after them. Of course, she'd paid the color consultant two hundred dollars an hour. That role was a skilled position. Nobody's born knowing what goes with mocha.

Occasionally Margo caught herself feeling smug that she treated the Guatemalan woman generously. Paying an unskilled illegal a decent amount was better than nickel-and-diming but was not going to change the course of society. Margo knew that if she was called before her Maker and asked to account for her life, leading with "I gave my cleaning woman more than my neighbors gave theirs" would be unlikely to open doors.

"Do you want a cappuccino? The machine does those, too," Margo said. She'd put on a tracksuit after her shower, and looked athletic. Setting about to install the new part in the machine in hopes of producing a cappuccino, she seemed the picture of competence. In a moment Margo began swearing like a sailor as steam blasted in the wrong direction—she had set one of the dials improperly.

Margo once passed an agreeable morning counting the controls and dials on her technological possessions. There were sixty-two switches with more than a hundred possible settings in the Lexus, and that wasn't including the hundreds of stations on the satellite radio. There were twenty-eight switches on the Bosch dishwasher. Her laptop, driven by software, could be set in essentially unlimited ways—and the moment she finally grasped current systems, upgrades forced her to start over. Margo tried to disable upgrades so the laptop would stay the same. But if she forgot and left the laptop on, the machine upgraded itself, mischievously, in the middle of the night. Too bad the laptop didn't make shoes while she was sleeping and leave them on the garage workbench.

Lillian watched, fascinated, as Margo confronted the cappuccino machine. This was something Lillian would never consider attempting herself, yet took on faith that a total stranger, earning minimum wage, would do correctly for her in a restaurant. Lillian lived alone, and made herself nothing more challenging than toast. Within walking distance of her downtown condo there were, after all, a profusion of interesting eating places, from quick American to elegant Northern Italian, plus every Asian, Central American and African subcuisine. Tea and a slice of toast with jam were all Lillian Epperson needed to start her day. Something better always came along later.

Margo had been born in Winnetka, Illinois, and raised in the kind of hopeful household that was drawing on two energies—the industrious hum of Chicago to the south and the peaceful murmur of Lake Michigan to the east. The sense of unlimited promise is trusted to all who come from the American Midwest, a place that was strong enough to resist an ice age. As a girl, Margo played on Tower Road Beach and liked gazing off into the distance, trying to spy where the lake ended. She assumed the water went on forever. In a sense this was true, since the water that now appeared to her as a lake had existed since shortly after the cosmos began and would continue to exist long after people were extinct or had evolved to some higher form.

Children born into circumstances where there is food and play but no war think the world was created to receive them personally. Margo as a girl thought this. For all we know, she was right.

Becoming a woman, Margo spent a few years on her own in the city, living in Lincoln Park, going to the music clubs and to watch experimental theater groups perform in converted auto-repair shops. She took lakeside walks with a succession of young men who collectively were somewhat above average in appeal. Lincoln Park was a comforting place—gentrified, with most residents headed upward in life, yet sufficiently urban and funky as to feel uncompromised. It was a privilege to have spent young adulthood there.

As for the apartment, she told her mother the building had been recommended by a good friend who knew the owner. Actually she'd found it by walking through neighborhoods until she passed a blocky tan structure with an APARTMENTS FOR RENT INQUIRE WITHIN sign by the entrance. Standing on the far side of the street for an hour, she observed the comings and goings of young men and women who seemed at approximately her station in life, which told her this was the spot. Margo worried about being conspicuous, that she would draw attention by lingering at the same location on an urban street for an hour. Instead not a single person looked twice at her, nor would have even if she'd been stealing tires or assembling a sniper rifle. But she was then only a few years removed from home—still at the point of assuming her every action was noticed.

Years later she would sometimes dream of her bachelorette apartment on West Belden Avenue. In her dreams, Margo saw not the boys who'd been her guests but the view through the window across West Belden to townhouses, the kind lived in by young couples who had gotten married and begun to make decent money.

Margo found a job as a trader's aide in the controlled chaos that is the Chicago Board Options Exchange—buying and selling not just the stocks of companies, which was comprehensible, but indices, swaps and spiders based on the stocks of companies. After a while she stopped thinking about what the indices and exchange-traded funds represented and cared only whether they went up or down: the attitude taken by the traders who were making the most money. Our distant forebears cultivated grasses into wheat; our nearer ancestors hewed land for farms; nearer still built factories, canals and bridges. The best-paid people of Margo's generation manipulated decimal points. Maybe this was a necessary stage in evolution to a higher form.

A regular habit was lunchtime Loop strolls. When

the winter gusts blew, she would go a short distance among the tall buildings that accelerated the wind. In warm weather, she would walk to the Chicago River, which had progressed from the filthy flammable sewer of Upton Sinclair's day to its current status of favored locale for dinner-boat cruises. When Margo worked there, Loop Chicago still had independent coffee shops on every block—the old urban kind that meant a counter serving cheeseburgers and grilled cheese sandwiches, a takeout line for coffee, the place passed down by a family. This was just before Starbucks invaded, with its diabolical marketing formula of double the price for twice the wait.

One day Margo collided in a coffee shop with a young man, spilling her coffee on his shirt. Better his shirt than her dress, all things considered. The collision felt nice. They joked a bit. As she was about to walk back to work, Margo stalled, wondering if he would ask for her phone number. He asked for her phone number, meaning the number at her apartment, of a desk phone attached to an answering machine with reel-to-reel magnetic tape. This being before even children carried global communication consoles.

Tom Helot, a business-school graduate, was charming, even-tempered and motivated. He was born in

Cooperstown, New York, a town that sits at the foot of a lake that is the source of the Susquehanna. Thus he shared with Margo a childhood fascination with distant waters, though not her illusions about them, since from any point along Otsego Lake, one can see the opposite shore. When school is out, Cooperstown and its environs bustle with tourists: the Finger Lakes area is in summer a cool, inviting fairyland. During winter the town clears and those who reside year-round struggle with snow and closed businesses. Tom felt grateful to have been a boy there, but wanted a bigger stage.

Margo liked hearing him talk of his ambitions—they would become well-to-do, they would use wealth responsibly, they would build a summer house on Keuka, the prettiest of the Finger Lakes, and make campfires with their children at the water's edge.

Margo believed there are three basic types of romances: the kind where passion rules, the kind that people fall into as the path of least resistance and the kind where people are made for each other. Passion-rules is a nice archetype. There was a boy in high school Margo could not keep her hands off. She couldn't have kept her hands off him if he had been on fire. But she could hardly stand him. Passion is a relief from reality, pushing out other thoughts. Romances based on passion have a poor track record, except in cinema.

Path-of-least-resistance causes the majority of human pairings, and after all, what did you expect? More or less falling into a relationship is better than loneliness, though has never inspired an epic poem. Margo's favorite band of her college years, Inane Pabulum, recorded a song that made her laugh, "More of Same," about the path-of-least-resistance relationship. The lyrics included:

That night when I first saw your face
I thought we'd met in some previous place
Was it because of your fair beauty
Or because life is all a blur to me?

More of same, more of same
"It's been done" is the modern refrain
I'm not new and neither are you
Life is just more of same.

When I asked you to dance you were unsurprised
I drunk deep of that jaded look in your eyes
You barely seemed to notice my charms
At least you stayed conscious in my arms.

More of same, more of same
Everyone rides on a scheduled train
I'm not new and neither are you
Our love is just more of same.

Had it come to that, Margo would have settled for more of same. But she believed the least likely type of romance—meant-to-be—is possible, and Tom was her proof.

As they began to date, Margo was able to imagine herself moving with him into one of the townhomes across West Belden. Tom's confidence, his optimism, that he never, ever complained—all seemed the right match. Margo and Tom both lost their fathers young, Tom's mother went early into dementia and Margo's mother had already been diagnosed with the cancer that would take her before she could see her grand-children. In that way too, Margo felt they were right for each other. The only family they would have in the future would be the one they made, and they would have only themselves to fall back on. After a court-ship, they were married at a country club that rented space for weddings. They began life together.

Having reset the cappuccino machine half a dozen times, finally confident the settings were correct,

Margo initiated an impressive sequence of grinding, steam, hissing and heat. When she set the cup under the spout, the new part flew skyward under pressure as the entire device did a passable imitation of a typical day at the Three Mile Island nuclear power station.

"No problem," Margo said as she and Lillian laughed. "I bought this American Express. They'll ship a replacement by next day."

Chapter 3

October 2007

Dow Jones Index: 14,000.

Unemployment: 4.6 percent.

National debt: $9.5 trillion.

The Helot children, Caroline and Megan, perceived the world in no small part through the windows of automobiles. Endless driving: to school, home, then back to school for extracurriculars; to oboe lessons, piano lessons and fencing lessons; to rock-climbing on synthetic materials manufactured to appear to be actual rocks; to orthodontists; many, many times to clothing stores, including to exchange items that had gone out of fashion before the girls could wear them to school; to tutors and to doctors' appointments; to soccer and to basketball.

Fencing lessons might have seemed a bit much, but Margo read somewhere that Ivy League colleges have trouble recruiting for fencing. For the team sports, invariably the girls had games on opposite ends of the county at the same time.

Margo made color-coded day planners to ensure Caroline and Megan would be in the right place, and toyed with the idea of shrinking the day planners into ones that moms could wear on their wrists, the way quarterbacks wear the plays. There might be a market for suburban-mom wrist-worn day organizers. A mom could flip one open, check the code numbers and colors and quickly call out, "Church bake sale on two. Hike!"

Things only seemed worthwhile if you had to drive to them. Every weekend at least one of the girls was invited to a birthday party, sometimes two, as if modern children were celebrating their birthdays biannually. Nobody held a party at the house anymore— birthday parties needed to be "events," which meant driving to a water park or laser tag or a magic show. Plus driving beforehand to get the presents. Margo wanted to start the year buying gift cards in bulk to wrap as presents when needed. Her girls were shocked by that; gifts had to be chosen person-by-person the day before a party, notwithstanding they almost always ended up buying gift cards. Every birthday party invitation represented at least two hours of driving.

"When we have our retirement home and ask each other, 'Where did the years go,'" Margo told Tom, "the answer will be that we spent them in the car."

She was pleased to drive a Lexus, though Margo never would have confessed that. Having a fancy car is nice: desiring one is shallow. Margo's was Blue Onyx Pearl with hand-stitched leather, though of course she had no way to know whether the stitching was done by well-paid workers with union protection in a modern factory or subcontracted to a developing-world sweatshop. Margo didn't want the gold badges, but the dealer threw them in.

Did driving-to-this, driving-to-that represent fun for the girls or would they rather have been left to their own accords to play in the woods, as was the case with previous generations?

This question was irrelevant for many contemporary families, because the spontaneous passage of youth, especially of summer, had given way to structure. Finding old clothes and declaring them the costumes of castle-games had been supplanted by parties with purchased costumes bearing trademarks. Spur-of-the-moment contests had been supplanted by organized leagues with start times and rulebooks. The monkey bars at the park playgrounds had been removed so there was nothing to fall off. Margo never would have considered allowing her daughters to frolic alone at the lakeshore, as she did in girlhood. Caroline and Megan inhabited a world in which the extemporaneous had been supplanted by the planned, and traditional risk had been reduced to the lowest possible level. Though innovative new risks were thriving quite nicely.

It was Friday; Margo was having a few people over—Lillian; Tom's business partner, Ken Afreet; and his wife, Nicole. Margo had always been uncomfortable with Ken, who was too open about his affection for money. Stress about money defines our age: but if you have enough, then stop complaining. Margo felt dismay that those she knew who had plenty in the bank nonetheless talked almost continuously about ways to get more. The best part about having money, Margo supposed, would be no longer thinking or caring about money. The people who had it did not respond that way.

Ken sure could run a business, though. Corsair Assets was on its fourth consecutive record year. Ken taught Tom much of what he knew about the private-equity field. He chose Tom to be the one who went around to the firms Corsair was acquiring, to assure the employees their jobs wouldn't vanish. Often the jobs vanished anyway, but that came later, and was due to market forces. Nicole had amusement value; she was trying hard to carry herself as a trophy wife so that she did not get replaced by an actual trophy wife. Nicole and Lillian were not a good mix, though. Lillian thought Nicole an airhead; Nicole thought Lillian an egghead. Both were right, but that wasn't the point. Men who clash can release the tension by insulting each other's sports teams. With women who clash, sooner or later it becomes personal.

Margo loved having people over, the sound of the front door opening and closing, cold air falling off the coats of friends who had just come in. Her neighborhood was of the kind that neighbors did not just wander by; people always called first, and drove even if they lived within a block.

Soon the girls would be teens, shuttling in and out with a floating cast of friends. Margo couldn't wait. For tonight, the children were in the finished basement watching movie rentals with a sitter, a highschool junior who charged twenty dollars an hour. Margo hustled to book the girl a week in advance, and felt lucky to have her. Most teens from the area didn't need walking-around cash, feeling no incentive to babysit or work the counter at Baskin-Robbins after school. Their parents simply fulfilled their every need, conferring on them more money and material things than seemed wise. Margo fought the urge to think the words "These kids today."

Perhaps being spoiled in youth is good, as long as the system that creates the spoiling will always function. Besides, if kids worked in ice-cream parlors or as baggers after school, they'd be taking wages from adults trying to support families. Immigrants and the unemployed formed lines for jobs at Burger King. Forty hours per week at the federal minimum wage left a head of household below the poverty line. Margo and her friends talked about the Oscars, celebrity sex scandals and foreign-policy blunders—they didn't talk about one American in eight being in poverty. There was upside: lots of adults seeking low-wage positions meant pizza delivery would be fast and yardwork cheap.

Awaiting her guests, Margo was on the phone talking to a friend and also intently inspecting her laptop. This is what you would have overheard if you were the nosy sort.

"Okay, January is out. There's so much picking up from the holidays anyway. You spend a month preparing for something that's over in thirty minutes, then the kids say, 'Is that all?' Let's look at February. Can't do the first weekend. The next weekend we're skiing in Utah depending on depth. Not that weekend either; I'm in San Francisco, then Tom is in London. During the week? Monday nights are my kickboxing class, the teacher is an ex-Marine with ripped abs. Sure you could come along!"

She paused to listen, then resumed: "Tuesday, Tom plays basketball. Wednesday night is PTA. Can't miss it." If asked, Margo would have explained that at-home moms needed to be present in force at the PTA to outvote the professional moms. That way the at-homes could deliberately schedule school events in the afternoon, forcing the professional moms to leave work early. The at-home mothers considered it essential to generate guilt in the professional mothers, if only to have a point on which to feel self-righteous. Margo was uneasy with this, but determined to maintain her influence with the PTA. That meant putting up with the bitchy moms—a substantial faction in any affluent community—who spent their days trying to think of something to complain about.

Back to her call: "Thursdays are out, peak homework night. Parents were saying academics weren't strict enough, teachers took their revenge by assigning more homework because they know the parents are really doing it. Friday nights Tom just collapses. I mix him his martini and he can barely lift it. Microwave martinis? I hadn't heard. March is tricky, spring sports leagues start. Let's look at April. No, can't do that day. I'm meeting with the college admission consultant. Megan is eleven, can't start too early. May is—damn, can you hold a minute?"

The friend said something. "I hate call-waiting too," Margo replied. "The only benefit of call-waiting is that you can be rude to two people simultaneously. But that's productivity, right?"

She took the new call, asking, "Is there a problem?" Margo began to speak very slowly, as if verbally capitalizing words. "On the Alaskan-southwestern pizza, half an order of grilled halibut and one order of twice-marinated grilled carne asada steak." Everyone said "grilled carne asada steak" though "*carne asada*" means grilled steak. "No. Not a double order of halibut and two orders of steak, that comes to four orders. Half an order of fish and one order of meat. No, not a double half order of each. Half an—" Switching to a language similar to Spanish, she said, placing emphasis on "supervisor": "*¿May excuzzo, puedo hablar por favor votre supervisor?*"

There was a pause as someone else came on the

phone. "Yes, we want a half an— You know what? Just substitute the blackened mango trout burritos, okay?"

Margo returned to the first call. "You were surfing with your phone while you waited? That's great. I can't watch movies on my phone—my phone is so old-fashioned. Okay, we're into June. Bad month, end-of-school-year events plus band concerts. Then camp driving starts. June twenty-seventh, we could do a late brunch, say one forty-five, but we'd have to be finished by three. You're already booked those hours? What about Fourth of July, have you got plans? We could do a picnic, you think? Okay, I've put you down for picnic on the Fourth of July. Call me around Valentine's Day to see if we're still on. Bye-bye."

Lillian knocked at the door, and Margo was glad to behold her. Scripture talks of countenance. To Margo, her friend had a countenance to behold, rather than a face to be seen.

Lillian complimented the new furniture, ordered in a custom brocade. Margo mentioned the price and her friend was shocked. "Every month the American Express bill is bigger than the mortgage," Margo explained.

"According to the newspapers, that makes you a patriot," Lillian replied.

Lillian had grown up on Long Island, and though her New York twang was lost in years of studying abroad, still called her hometown region *long-GUY-land*, as if with a liaison. An only child, she came from a forlorn household where almost every night the shouting between her father and mother would begin at nine P.M., as if cued by some unseen, sadistic theatrical director. She learned early to retreat and cower. It was almost worse because the shouting had nothing to do with the child, her parents being so wrapped up in their rituals of grievance against each other, they barely seemed aware Lillian could hear their screamed denigration. Some blame the world for their problems, some blame themselves, others blame whomever is closest. Lillian's parents fell into the latter category. When she left for college, Lillian did not come home for summers or holidays. After the first year, her parents didn't ask her to.

She did well in graduate school, then landed a tenure-track teaching job on her first try. It helped to have an obscure specialty, so no one else on the faculty could be sure whether you knew what you were talking about. Initially Lillian was surprised to find herself surrounded by others with stories of terrible growing-up situations. First she thought the other college professors who told tales of woe about childhood merely were engaging in the contest of fashionable gloom that is upper academia. Then Lillian began to realize large numbers of people were unhappy about their childhoods, at least in retrospect. Many felt their one shot at carefree youth had been stolen from them by callous adults, skipping over the fact that the callous adults were in most cases the same people who gave them their one shot at carefree youth by sacrificing their own one shot at carefree middle age.

People who looked back in anger on childhood hailed from all walks of life. But only small numbers— writers, professors, TV personalities—were in positions to make their dissatisfaction known. Eventually Lillian came to feel that many who talked obsessively about childhood disappointments weren't really choleric about their cold parents or nasty teachers or the cliquish cool kids in high school or the football coach who didn't let them play or the drama teacher who didn't cast them in the school show. What they were mad about was life: which starts off without responsibilities or disappointments, then becomes one bummer after another. Realizing this, Lillian henceforth kept her feelings about her early years to herself.

She settled into adulthood reasonably smoothly, other than disliking weekends. Weeknights she enjoyed: on them, she was expected to be concerned about work, and to hit the sack early. Friday and Saturday nights, when you're supposed to be invited to something and stay out late, Lillian could have done without.

Having mentioned newspapers, Lillian picked up that morning's from a sideboard. The headlines concerned a political scandal: furious accusations, heated denials, a commission appointed. The whole matter certainly sounded shocking.

"I read the story and by the end wasn't sure what, exactly, the senator was accused of," Lillian said.

"Oh, I love political scandals," Margo declared with an enthusiasm that was genuine. "When I lived in Chicago, there was always a new one. Each day you'd think, 'It's finally happened, every possible form of graft has been tried.' Then you'd wake up the next morning, unfold the paper, and discover some completely new venality. Reassuring, in a way—to realize there would never be any limit to the ability of the human mind to devise ways to cheat."

"Reporters seem to live for scandals."

"Chance to be negative, every journalist's dream," Margo said.

"I went out with a reporter once," Lillian said. Her former boyfriends were a regular topic of conversation, and if there was one who did not deserve to be in the dock at The Hague, Lillian had not gotten to him. "From *The Washington Post*," she continued. "He was very aggressive—kept asking about my finances. In restaurants, he looked at other women while he talked to me. Once I asked how he can be so sure of his stories and he said, 'We always have two sources for every fact we distort.' I had to point out that he meant report, not distort.'"

"They're such similar words."

"Yes, aren't they."

The front door opened again and Tom, Ken and Nicole entered. Tom was good-looking and outgoing, never testy, the kind of person who is expected by those around him to do well. He seemed to have something important on his mind even when he did not. Since his youth, when people he knew were unsure on some question or small controversy, they'd say, "Let's ask Tom."

Margo always felt better when he was near. She could sense Tom's presence in the house: not that she'd hear him talking or walking—she'd know. When Tom was out of town she would take one of his T-shirts from the laundry basket, unwashed, and sleep in it, because it smelled like him.

"Even huge as that thing is, you can just nail people at stoplights," Ken was saying. They were animated and speaking loudly, as if they'd just come from a rock concert or rodeo or similar high-energy event.

"Yeah? Fast?" Tom asked.

"Mojo fast. Plus people get out of your way. I had the dealer install extra-bright high beams and blackout windows to make it look menacing. When you're in something that big and fast, you cut people off anytime you want."

"Ken likes to cut people off," Nicole noted.

"Your SUV sounds great," Tom said. "But don't you worry about global warming?"

"Sure—I worry global warming won't happen fast enough for those lakefront acres I bought in Buffalo to become a play. If the climate warms like they're predicting, in twenty years Buffalo will have ideal weather. Millionaires will build vacation homes there and sip wine as they watch the sun set behind the abandoned slag towers. I'm on the ground floor of that land rush. Anyway, if I don't waste gasoline, somebody else will."

Ken turned to Lillian, who walked the city and bicycled around the campus, but kept a tiny, high-mileage compact of the type that resembles a Flintstones car with a hole at the bottom to pedal using your feet. Lillian used it on weekends and to drive to Margo's, always feeling a wave of trepidation when she left the downtown streets and joined a freeway to the suburbs, the traffic moving so, so fast.

"Lilly," Ken told her, "get rid of that hybrid and put yourself in something that seats eight. It's survival of the fittest out there on the road. If Charles Darwin were here, he would be first in line at the dealership for an SUV, I'm telling you."

She disliked being addressed as Lilly. "SUVs are irresponsible and dangerous," she said.

Ken replied, "That's the whole point!"

Tom kissed Margo, who explained there was a foul-up with the delivery because she was taking a flyer on the new Alaskan-Mexican place. They'd had so much Tex-Mex and Cal-Mex, she wanted to try AK-Mex.

"A Thai-Lebanese tapas restaurant just opened near my apartment," Lillian said. She often ordered out, believing food tastes better when it's cooked by someone you have never met. Margo had been in Lillian's apartment and was worried to discover the refrigerator contained only yogurt and fruit. To Margo, a dwelling should be well stocked with meats, cheeses, pastas, milk, juices, breads, vegetables, beer and whiskey. But then she had children and a husband; Lillian had neither. Besides, there were dozens of restaurants within walking distance of Lillian's place, and she enjoyed taking her meals out, including breakfast and afternoon tea. Being handed a menu Lillian found to be one of life's consistent pleasures.

"Who wants wine?" Margo asked, giving Tom a bottle to open. The vintage was recommended by a gourmet magazine. Margo received several, though she'd never subscribed to any. Gourmet magazines just arrive at the house if you're spending enough. Somehow they know.

"I love those magazines, I always clip the recipes Ken would like," Nicole said. She was perfectly turned out, and wore high heels even when no one else was present. "I never actually cook the recipes for Ken, but at least I have them." Her husband laughed in a vigorous way. He liked Nicole to seem flighty. If Nicole had wanted to discuss, say, the state of emergency just declared in Pakistan, that would have upset Ken. Not the subject, rather that Nicole showed an interest in it.

The restaurant called with word the deliveryman would be late. "What assholes," Ken said.

Tom had put himself through college with numerous odd jobs, including as a pizza driver, and so was offended by this comment. He proposed there should be sympathy for deliverymen—it's a hard way to make ends meet. "Delivery work is real work," Tom said. "And the car is your own; if it breaks down, that wipes out a week's wages."

"What is hard about sitting on a seat and pressing a pedal?" Ken asked. "The poor of the past did backbreaking labor in the sun. Today a poor person can earn tips driving an air-conditioned car, then stop someplace for a double burger with free extra fries." Nicole looked on her husband admiringly as he continued, "The land of opportunity! Supersizing, jobs with no immigration status check—just two of the reasons half the world is trying to sneak across our borders."

Experience had taught that it would be only a matter of moments until Ken began to discourse on government selling out the nation to the Muslims and the gays. Ken, who cheated on his taxes and had never once made the effort to vote, possessed high standards regarding how everyone else should serve the country. Margo changed the subject by asking Tom if the quarterly numbers had come in.

"They were supposed to, but it's looking like Monday. We're expecting a big stock-price bump when these numbers are announced." Corsair had gone public, and Tom exercised the large number of share options granted him years before when the firm was a startup. With the company's price rising, he thought the timing was right to sell the shares and take his profit. Margo had been urging him to do so.

The unsold shares were a ghostly presence in their lives. As farm wives and husbands argue about what day on which to sell the crop to the co-op, Tom and Margo argued about when to cash out the shares. For two years Margo had wanted to sell, bank whatever money the stock would fetch and solidify the family's future. She knew that, like the country, they were living well but not saving. Millions of Americans were spending as if tomorrow would never come. Tomorrow has a way of coming.

Tom wanted to bide their time and let the price run up. Now, with the stock market hitting an all-time high, he thought the moment had arrived. Margo was delighted by his decision, just reached, to start selling the shares.

"So the company's in good shape," Lillian said.

"Fantastic. Five years ago we had a handful of people working in a converted warehouse with pull-grate elevators. Now we're a listed company with two hundred and ninety employees in three states and almost $30 billion under management. America—this is the country of up. Living standards, life spans, profits— everything goes up." Ken was scowling as Tom spoke.

"Skirts certainly go up," Margo said. "I had Caroline and Megan at the mall after school. It terrifies me how little the high-school girls are wearing, and that's what Caroline and Megan admire."

"Up, up, up," Tom said. "Each generation has more than the generation before, and I don't think that's ever going to end. When our parents were young, a bungalow house and a car, that was the American Dream. Now the average home is four bedrooms and the average family has three cars. That's the average!" Tom was delighted by that statistic. "The only direction this country can go is up." He put his arms around Margo. "Starting Monday, I will sell the legal maximum of our shares. You and I and the girls will be set for life."

"You never know about stock prices," Ken said. "The market is fickle." He made the comment sound oily.

"You're the one who talked me out of selling six months ago!" Tom laughed. "You said I'd do much better to wait a little longer."

The doorbell rang, signaling the arrival of the deliveryman. Tom paid. Ken opened a second bottle of wine.

"I hope you didn't tip too much," Nicole said. She viewed tipping people in everyday circumstances as a complete waste of money: they would never see that deliveryman again; she would never see a waitress or hotel car valet again, so why hand them money? Then at wedding receptions or other society events where her social acquaintances were present she would hand out twenties as if they were gumdrops, waving them first in order to be noticed.

"Tom always tips too much," said Margo. When they were dating, she wondered if he was trying to impress her. But he kept up tipping too much after marriage. Margo added, "And Tom gives dollar bills to the homeless men who stand at intersections and beg from cars stopped at red lights."

"Some guy standing at an intersection holding a foam cup, he needs a dollar bill more than I do."

"But you have to roll down the window," Margo said. "It's creepy."

"In a free country," Nicole said, "if you don't have money, you must blame yourself. That's one of the great things about America."

Tom had long since stopped trying to reason with Nicole, and so addressed the others: "As long as we are paying a large amount to a distant company, that's fine. But hand a buck to another human being, that's strange."

"When you cash out your shares, why don't you downshift?" Lillian suggested. "Move to a college town in some leafy place, live on half as much. Sit on the porch and watch the sunset."

Margo sometimes thought about the downshifting alternative, which held obvious appeal. "Tom and I talk about the small-town existence; it's attractive," she said. "But suppose we lived in some idyllic Berkshires town, I'd worry constantly we weren't giving every possible opportunity to the girls. Plus if I ever actually felt content, that itself would worry me."

She laughed, and looked prettier when she did so—her pretty laugh was among the things that had attracted Tom. "When we're on vacation and the stress stops, for the first few days I feel great. Then I feel like

I'm missing something—like I'm supposed to feel stress."

Lillian had recently attended a lecture on this very point. "Natural selection designed you to be discontent," she said. "Stress is nature's way. The wary of the primordial past, the ones always scanning the horizon for predators and never satisfied no matter how much they accumulated—those are the ones who survived and passed their dispositions down to us. Our happy-go-lucky ancestors stopped to smell the flowers and got eaten by something. If we are descended from the stressed-out of the past, then evolution has been encouraging nervous tension." The Galápagos finches got ever-sharper beaks. People get ever more stress.

Margo laughed anew; she was pleased when her friend sounded like a college professor. Too often, Lillian seemed not confident about who she was.

"So you're saying that in natural-selection terms, I pass my melancholy along to my daughters, who will evolve it into a more complex form of discontentedness?"

"Today's complaints are much more elaborate than the complaints of our distant ancestors," Lillian said. "This is one of the achievements of Western civilization."

"Natural selection wants us to be nasty—I like that," Ken said, jumping to an entirely different conclusion. "I can use that at the emerging-markets conference. The business world is kill or be killed, just like a PBS nature special. To feel content is a bad strategy, a competitive disadvantage. Render the competition extinct. Good stuff."

Nicole was dismayed the conversation was turning philosophical. At the country club, that never happened.

"If you feel constant discontent, aren't you only cheating yourself?" Tom asked. "So many people—they've got a nice house, they're healthy, and all they think about is what they don't have. Or about some imagined slight or trivial grudge. Who are they harming but themselves? People spend too much time discussing material things, not enough appreciating this life we grasp so briefly. At the ends of our lives, will we even remember what we possessed?"

Ken: "Absolutely!"

"Lillian may be right about the quiet college-town life. I wish I watched the sun rise more often," Tom said. When she started spending the night at Tom's place, Margo had been charmed that he sometimes rose early, to watch the dawn.

Tom asked Ken, "How often do you watch the daily miracle of the sunrise?"

Ken hated when Tom sounded like this, though knew Tom's pensive side helped close more than one deal. Endowment funds loved the way he talked.

Normally Ken would change the subject when Tom grew reflective, but he couldn't stand to be perceived as having lost a debating point. Ken said, "Now you want me to feel thankful there's sunlight? How about oxygen and nitrogen, people should feel thankful for them? And magnesium, let's see a little gratitude for the daily miracle of magnesium."

Nicole blanched on the word "magnesium." Saying, "Normal people do not discuss science at parties," she went into the den and turned on the television, choosing a popular show on which magazine-cover fashion models competed to find faults in one another.

In the current episode, the task was to damage the other models' reputations. At the end of each episode there were two audience votes via an 800 line—ubiquitous texting hadn't quite yet happened. The first concerned which model would be thrown off the show for being revealed to have a fault. In the second vote, whichever model had been perceived by the audience as "too nice," for not being sufficiently heartless against the others, would also be expelled from the show. That was Nicole's favorite part. Focus groups run by the network showed viewers really liked that part too.

Margo and Lillian continued talking in the kitchen. Ken and Tom took their wine out onto the deck, which Tom had added during the deck fad. He was thinking of adding an outdoor fireplace, the current high-end home fad.

"I had lunch with Gresham Cooper yesterday," Tom said. "He's been named senior partner. We made a bet on which of us will retire before fifty."

"Cooper is a terrific lawyer. I didn't even know I had legal problems until I hired him," Ken replied. "Except his plastic surgeon did too good a job. You can't tell he had his eye wrinkles removed."

"Isn't that the desired outcome?"

"When a woman has cosmetic surgery, the point is to look better. For a man, the point is to announce to the world that you've got the bucks to afford cosmetic surgery and you've reached the kind of power position in life where simulating youth gives you an advantage. So you need the facial fixes to be obvious. Otherwise, how will anyone know?"

Ken sipped wine from the new bottle. "This is nice; write down the name for me and I'll get a case."

He had just purchased a SubZero wine-storage unit and needed to fill it. There was space for 147 bottles, different temperatures for Burgundy and Bordeaux. Six thousand dollars, plus installation cost. The unit was so heavy, installers had to reinforce the floor.

"How much do you think our stock price will go up when the numbers come out?"

Ken tried to raise other subjects, including sports, cars and babes, the perennials of male conversation. Finally he said, "Investors—they're capricious. Anyway, we put too much score by Wall Street. We should get back to what originally made this country strong, like land speculation."

"You are awfully downbeat when we're about to announce a record quarter."

Ken had a way of seeming bitter and cheerful both at once: a good mix for business success. "In this day and age we've become too good at being phony," he said. "We're so efficient at phony, people are suspicious when something is real. Plus the bigger a faker you are, the higher your take. Because society rewards phoniness, we get more of it—I mean, that's textbook economics."

Tom was not sure why matters such as this should be on Ken's mind. Ken had seemed distracted in the last few days, but everyone has phases like that. Yesterday, Tom mentioned to him what seemed like a potentially lucrative acquisition and Ken hadn't been interested, which was like a bear not being interested in salmon.

Ken gave Tom a distressed look and asked, "Did you ever break it off?"

Tom didn't know what Ken meant.

"Ask some chick to marry you, choose the date, meet the 'rents, start making arrangements, then have to go say, 'Sorry, cupcake, I found somebody better-looking, I'm breaking it off.'"

"I never did any such thing," Tom said, as if answering a homeroom teacher.

"Well, I did three times and I am here to tell you it's no walk in the park. And that's how I feel right now."

The deck was a pleasant place on which to stand; you felt elevated. Every ninety seconds a jetliner arced overhead, inbound to the airport. Early in the morning and early in the evening—rush hours occur at airfields, too—in good weather the planes were only thirty seconds apart, the minimum safe separation. Americans need to get where they need to go. Each plane, landing, had to turn off the runway onto a taxiway the moment it was capable of doing so, to prevent the next arrival from overrunning the previous.

Tom demanded that Ken say what was on his mind.

"It's time I was totally frank with you," Ken replied. Then he spoke in a synthetic tone, the way powerful people speak to a congressional committee when they've done something bad but know they will never be punished in any way: "There were regrettable oversights and inadvertent misstatements. There were lapses of judgment. Insufficient disclosure may have occurred. Monies may have been improperly diverted. Nonnominal transients may have eventuated. Mistakes may have been made. Frankly, I am going to be totally frank. Mistakes, in fact, were made."

Tom got it immediately. "So we're not about to announce record profits—we're about to announce a huge problem."

"The problem is we're bankrupt. The company is finished."

"But just last quarter our cash-on-hand—"

"Our cash reserve was a bookkeeping fiction, like most of our assets."

"But our accounts receivable, they were worth—"

As if reading a statement prepared by an attorney,

Ken said, "Regrettably, certain amounts may have been misdirected into special offshore entities that are unlikely to withstand regulatory scrutiny. Certain members of our board may be involved. I may be involved."

"Stop talking like that! Tell me what's going on."

"What's going on is that the directors and I looted the investors blind. I've lied to keep the investigators at bay for as long as I could. They found out. We are toast."

Tom tried to make himself think rationally, to avoid becoming emotional. "How did you get this past the accountants?" he asked.

Ken answered, "That was the easy part."

Tom's mind was reeling. Not only was his business partner a highwayman—bankruptcy would wipe out the value of his shares. "You're a thief," Tom said, not without difficulty. "You stole from our investors, who trusted us."

If he had a mustache, Ken might have twirled it. But Ken was not sorry to have broken the law: sorry only to have been caught. In this, he took the prevailing view embraced by white-collar criminals, corporate titans and government insiders.

"All I've done is what half the CEOs and Wall Street lions do," Ken said. "The members of the best clubs in Manhattan or Boston, the big political donors, the grandees on the Council on Foreign Relations— they got where they are by stealing from investors. It's the modern way! Plenty of America's corporate leaders belong in jail. But they're not, are they? They're in Aspen or Davos or a suite at Lake Tahoe with two honeys from a high-end Internet escort service. I'm just trying to emulate their success—I'm working within the system! The only difference between me and the business leaders who get invited to the White House is that they stole enough to become patrons of the arts. Anyway, I can still dream."

"I've been living a lie."

"Not you. You're so naive, you think so highly of human nature, you never guessed." Something repulsive flashed in Ken's eyes. "There were millions of dollars of other people's money in our investor accounts and it never occurred to you that the money might grow legs and walk away. That would be dishonest— that couldn't happen!"

Tom was speechless. Ken was bitter and cheerful.

"It's amazing how many people fall for this basic scam," he said. "Contractor tells the Pentagon that shipping supplies to Iraq will cost ten billion. Just never occurs to anyone that once that cash is in the account, most of it will be stolen. Some guy claims to have a miracle investing formula that guarantees outsized returns. People with big bucks hand over their dough, it never occurs to them that the money will be stolen. They never ask themselves, 'If this guy actually has a miracle wealth formula, why the fuck would he share it with me?' People with big bucks, you'd think they would be smart about money. They are the easiest ones to fool! They want to believe the system is rigged in their favor."

He paused, then continued: "You were easy to fool. Worked alongside me for years and had no clue." Ken was pleased that he had duped Tom so thoroughly—it made him feel like a master criminal. "Look on the bright side," he added. "You walk away an honest man."

"I was about to cash out—we would have made eight, maybe nine million dollars."

"By deceiving investors! Give me some credit, I saved you from that."

Now it dawned on Tom that if the firm's chief officer had been stealing all along, he would not have allowed the company to collapse without first getting his share. "How much did you divert to yourself?"

"I've never claimed to be burdened by ethics," Ken said. "I've never bragged about tipping the pizza guy."

"How much?"

"It is a fallacy that there are right and wrong levels of executive compensation. My compensation reflected market forces."

"But if the numbers were phony, you were—"

"Awarding myself huge bonuses for performance that was imaginary. That, my friend, is called vision! When artists become wealthy based on sheer imagination, this is admired. Andy Warhol made a killing by photocopying a soup can. That's vision! He had a dream, a dream that people would pay him lavishly for obvious crap. He made his dream come true. Why shouldn't we admire the businessman who achieves the same?"

Then Ken added, "I had the vision to sell most of my shares last year. You hesitated."

"You talked me out of selling last year!"

"Which was my fiduciary responsibility. If more shares had come onto the market, our stock price would have declined."

"When I get to the office Monday, the first thing I'm going to do is go to the files and—"

"You won't be in the office Monday," Ken said. "A few hours ago the board fired everyone except me. They invoked a clause in your contract that forbids you to step on company property. Can't have you making photocopies, pal. Security will call the police if you try to enter the office. Don't take it personal or anything."

Years of work gone in an instant, and Tom had never guessed what was happening.

In the back of his mind it had sometimes seemed too good to be true—revenue gushing in, numbers rising, stock analysts touting the firm; yet what was it, exactly, they created? He had tried not to think about the musical-chairs aspect of the modern financial industry. Presidents, prime ministers, governors, editorial writers, the *Harvard Business Review*—all were praising the financial sector as the growth engine of the West. But unlike carmakers or farmers who had inventories that could be inspected, financial firms asked you to take their numbers on faith. If the numbers were lies . . . Tom's head reeled with the realization that he had been part of such a lie, and too credulous to notice.

"We're sort of—delicately balanced, financially," Tom said. "I don't have a lot of savings. My contract calls for two years' salary if leaving the firm for any reason. I want those funds immediately."

"Bankruptcy voids financial promises that may have been made. No golden parachute. You can buy back your benefits, though. Keep the executive life insurance, so long as you make the payments. It's a very generous offer."

"Unbelievable."

Ken said, "You know, I don't have any trouble at all believing it."

Tom was silent. A few months before, he had been offered a senior position with a great package to join General Electric; Ken talked him out of it. Tom now realized Ken would have known then their enterprise was fixed and sure to fail. Ken didn't just steal from the investors, he stole from Tom. Wiped out, and a fool to boot.

"Many business-school success stories lost their shirts at some point—maybe that can be you," Ken said, trying to sound soothing. "We live in a fast, flexible, kanban, six-sigma economy. To achieve maximum throughout, people must be expendable. Besides, you've been expressing qualms about materialism. Now you'll get a nice break from that."

At that moment Tom felt glad there was no rifle in

the house, because he would have dropped Ken where he stood. Instead Tom said softly, "I will see to it that you end up in jail."

"No you won't, buddy boy. My tracks are covered. While you were philosophizing, I was taking care of Number One."

Tom had not punched anyone since a silly high-school rumpus that barely constituted a fight. He had, however, been in regular attendance in boxing aerobics at his health club: the woman who taught the class was good-looking and hardly wore anything. The haymaker hit Ken with such force, Tom was surprised he had delivered the blow so effectively.

Sitting by the kitchen island having an agreeable conversation, Margo and Lillian did not hear the sound of a guest falling unconscious onto the deck. Making popcorn to take into the basement for the girls and the sitter, they were discussing how at times like this, life seems perfect.

Outside the wind rustled pleasantly through the trees as Tom's chest heaved from the exertion of the punch—every now and then he had a bit of trouble breathing. Ken's jaw was broken in four places. On advice of counsel he did not press charges, in order to avoid a situation in which Tom could hire an attorney who would receive court permission to engage in discovery. Nicole's favorite magazine-cover model contestant won the reality show episode by planting an Internet rumor that her rival made a sex tape with her personal trainer at Canyon Ranch. And Margo's life would stop being perfect.

Chapter 4

October 2008

Dow Jones Index: 8,000.
Unemployment: 6.6 percent.
National debt: $10.4 trillion.

From the office tower the view was of a frenzy of freeways: chock to the lane markers with cars, buses and trucks moving insistently, everyone wanting to be somewhere they were not. Watching so many vehicles in motion might be inspiring if the motion were purposeful. The traffic Tom saw from the office tower window was streaming along close together in space and time, as if someone had planned this outcome. You'd like to assume the traffic was acting out a plan. But there was no design. Each person behind a wheel was on his or her own, and none had the slightest idea what the next was doing, other than exhibiting nervous anxiety.

The companies and governments of the world—you'd like to assume they are working from a well-thought-out blueprint intended to keep things together. Perhaps that is too much to ask. You might be content to assume they are following a slapdash plan or even a dumb plan, as long as events are happening for a reason later to be revealed. You'd like to assume there is a person in charge in a master control room, turning dials—like Professor Marvel in *The Wizard of Oz*, or like in a James Bond movie. Maybe that person is the president or a billionaire banker. Maybe it's someone really powerful, like the CEO of Walmart.

Movies, thriller stories—there's always a hidden hand, a master villain, a secret committee orchestrating events. If there were a committee of illuminati covertly controlling world events, they aren't doing much of a job. But just as no one was in charge of the mess on the freeways, no one is in charge of the international economy. The president, the chair of the Federal Reserve, the military-industrial complex, those European bankers with their fine Champagnes—nobody has control over the economy, which autonomously does what it is supposed to do: increases the output of goods and services without regard to individual welfare. It's not that the plan isn't working. There is no plan.

Tom looked for a moment at the view, reflecting that in less than a year he'd slipped from a plush corner office at a firm that was a Wall Street darling, to a small office with no window at General Electric head-quarters in Connecticut while he was a contract hire filling a six-month post, to a cubicle at the Internet start-up ZiZi, which hoped to allow people to broadcast personal television networks using smart phones.

In the wake of the financial market freeze that began in September 2008, ZiZi went out of business. Tom was now helping place what was left of the company into boxes so ZiZi could vacate the premises. He unplugged high-tech servers, stuffed with advanced microscopic circuits whose function hardly anyone understands, surrounded them with bubble wrap and placed them into shipping containers. On one table was a large box of glossy pamphlets touting the new firm's generous pension plan, which now would never exist. There was a sticky note attached to the box, instructing that its contents be recycled.

A few months before this moment Tom had been called to the office of Jeff Immelt, CEO of General Electric. There was no reason for him to have facetime with the top executive unless he was being offered a senior position, a real post with security and benefits, not just an extension of his glorified-temp status. Tom's résumé showed him well qualified for a senior position, and he'd been receiving glowing evaluations in his current trial run. He walked happily through the broad, chrome-trimmed halls of General Electric headquarters, a building raised in an era when it was thought that major corporations would be more stable than nations.

Immelt's Chief of Staff met Tom in the executive reception area. He wasn't an assistant, he was the Chief of Staff, to whom a Deputy Chief of Staff reported. Even charities and think tanks were embracing such inflated White House–style titles.

Instead of escorting Tom in to see Immelt, the aide motioned him to a side room. "Change of plans," he said. "You're being let go."

Immediately Tom knew he never should have mentioned the appointment to Margo. Now he would seem at fault in some way, as if he'd blown his chance at a secure, high-paying job.

Tom tried responding in corporate psychobabble, of which there is a surprising amount. *We should empower the stakeholders by inviting them into the conversation* is the sort of thing modern corporate managers say when what they mean is, *Let's go through the motions of consulting community groups before we crush them.* Tom told the aide, "If there is a deficiency issue in my performance, I would be happy to discuss a remediation schedule."

"No, sorry, you're out," the aide replied. He wore his blue blazer indoors. Any place the CEO might stroll past, the men keep their sport coats on and the women keep on the jackets of their power suits, though Immelt himself walked around in khakis without a tie. Once suits meant you were the boss and jeans meant you were the help. Now jeans mean you are the boss.

"The board just imposed a white-collar slots freeze," the aide explained.

"But the stock market is in good shape, the GDP is solid, the Bear Stearns disintegration was just a bump in the road."

"Company internal analysis shows the U.S. economy is overextended. We are hunkering down." He paused. "The board feels it's better to let top people go now when they can find something, rather than wait till the recession hits."

"Recession!" Tom was shocked at that word. Stocks, real estate, banking—all had been go-go for years, with no clouds on the horizon. Hedge funds and private-equity managers were complaining they had so much liquid capital they couldn't find enough assets to invest in.

"I'm sorry that as a contract hire you don't have any vesting, which means no buy-out," the aide said. A Wharton grad carrying two mortgages—residence and vacation home—the boss's Chief of Staff seemed nervous, as if wondering how long till he, too, was motioned into a side office.

Tom was close to speechless, so listened as the aide laid it out for him: "Our internal data show a major housing bubble based on subprime liars' loans securitized into ersatz bonds—the buyers and the brokers are both cheating. Plus crazy-bad leverage at the big pin-striped Wall Street houses. Big financial firms are declaring paper profits based on debt swaps and derivatives that are phony as three-dollar bills. Top corporate bonuses are way too high—too high for the system to sustain itself, even if you don't care about stepping on the fates of average people. The hedge funds' big numbers are not coming from productive investments, the hedge funds are simply being used as covers for insider trading. Next there will be a huge run-up in federal borrowing for bailouts and giveaways to interest groups. The ratio of government debt to GDP will soar, unless the politicians show some courage, and can you name one politician in Washington who cares about anything other than personal power and campaign donations?"

The aide made a whisper motion, though no other person was present to overhear. "Mr. Immelt was in Washington last week and tried to talk to the treasury secretary about this. The treasury secretary got angry and practically threw Mr. Immelt out. The White House wants to cut taxes for the rich even more, and expand the Iraq War into Iran. No one in his right mind would do those things if a recession was coming."

A few months later, Treasury Secretary Henry Paulson would stand at the White House press room podium, visibly shaking, and say the American economy would collapse within days if Congress did not give a $700 billion bailout, without oversight, to big banks and Wall Street. Paulson would tell a journalist he picked $700 billion based not on econometric analysis but because he thought it was the highest number that would not make people laugh.

To work his contract job at the General Electric campus, Tom had been living in an extended-stay hotel, far from the family, and expensing the cost. On the day he was let go, he received a legal-looking notice saying the company would pay for one additional night in the hotel, but would charge him to ship home his box of miscellaneous office stuff. Page after page of tiny-type disclaimers followed the notice. He had to initial each page, as a General Electric lawyer watched.

Shortly after Tom was dismissed in Connecticut, the venture capital firm backing ZiZi called, and soon Tom was in another hotel far from wife and girls. The start-up's idea seemed weird, but so did the idea for the Kaypro, a 1980 invention that was the first computer light enough to carry. Who needed *that*? Tom grimaced when ZiZi offered him mainly stock options at a $1 strike price, little regular pay. The family was burning through savings fast—he wanted salary. But the lore of the high-tech economy is fired one day, rich the next. He took the offer and plunged into work, often at the office till ten P.M. then back at seven A.M. There was nothing at the hotel except watching television anyway.

In September 2008, Tom had been in Manhattan doing a road show with investment bankers. Start-ups meet with investment bankers to see which proposes the best terms to underwrite an initial public offering, and ZiZi was ready for its IPO. Ready financially and in terms of market buzz, at least: even ZiZi employees couldn't explain what a "personal television network" might be. If the IPO went according to

ZiZi's projections, Tom would become a millionaire after all.

In the morning, Tom and ZiZi's founder met some investment bankers who said the new company should be worth $1.2 billion. At that price, Tom's options would have left him, Margo, and the girls set for life. Then the investment bankers began gaping at the crawl on CNBC. Lehman Brothers, a citadel of money and privilege, had just admitted its books were cooked and gone bankrupt, the largest corporate failure in United States history.

Over lunch, another set of investment bankers said that considering the sudden equities downturn, ZiZi should have an initial capitalization of $400 million. Two-thirds lost in a few hours, but at that number, Tom, Margo and the girls still would be out of the woods. By late afternoon at the market close, the Dow Jones having fallen five hundred points in a single day, the last investment banking firm they called on said ZiZi was worthless. No one would buy any start-up equities until Wall Street recovered. A week later the venture capitalists, who lived in California beachfront homes and received million-plus bonuses for shuffling paperwork, pulled the plug on ZiZi, and Tom was unemployed again. The venture capitalists offered him a thousand dollars to help close down the firm. He accepted.

The man who founded ZiZi was the only other person left in the office, and like Tom, was filling boxes with leased equipment to ship back to a warehouse. He was fit and slender, slightly graying, turned out in khakis and unlaced Timberland boots such as pop stars wear, plus a plain white T-shirt that had cost him ninety dollars in a Beverly Hills boutique. Once in a while the office phone rang—someone asking if ZiZi was accepting job applications.

When the word had come from the venture capitalists about closing ZiZi, people in the office cried, or pounded their fists, or broke down. The firm's founder was blasé. He sat for a moment drumming his fingers, shrugged, then pulled a bottle of forty-year-old scotch from a desk drawer. He broke the capsule, opened the bottle and passed it around, with plastic cups. After the contents vanished, he produced another unopened bottle, that one fifty-eight years old, broke another capsule and passed more around. When Jesus turned water to wine, the wedding guests were amazed that the host had saved the best for last, rather than serving the good stuff first and then pouring cheap wine once everyone was drunk. If the host had said, "Actually, I ran out of wine, so the Son of God did me a favor by turning some rainwater into Chateau Montelena," who would have believed that story? Most likely Jesus, too, was drunk, the kind of point they tend to skip in church.

Involved in start-ups of a dozen firms, two of which were big moneymakers and the rest busts, ZiZi's founder lived his life in economic turbulence and considered this normal. He had moved in the last twenty-five years to New York, then Atlanta, then Chicago, then New York, then Palo Alto, then Falls Church, then Waltham, then Pasadena, then Seattle, then New York, then Seattle, then Menlo Park. Thrice divorced in the process, he rarely saw any of his several children. He'd made, lost and made again his fortune, owned a magnificent twenty-meter sailboat that he called "the raft," and kept up all support payments.

"Tom, help me with these," he said. There were numerous boxes, each containing twenty-four unopened BlackBerrys, intended to distribute to staff that was never hired. Though the devices had to be returned, most likely they would be written off and junked as already obsolete. Up in Canada, researchers were racing to add more keys to the next-gen Black-Berry. The thirty-eight keys, plus miniature joystick, weren't enough.

"We got screwed," Tom said, of nothing in particular.

"Luck is what it is," the man replied. "From Wall Street and romancing investors I've known some really rich people. They insist on believing they are rich due to their hard work, inspired ideas and superhuman personal merit. That way they can think it's fair that they have far more money than they will ever know what to do with, while others cry themselves to sleep at night over a few hundred bucks. The rich man wants to believe he's rich, and the poor are poor, based solely on what each deserved. Me, I acknowledge whether you become rich or poor is at least half luck. I've had good luck. With this start-up, we had bad luck. Whether your luck is good or bad, Tom, don't think either is any reflection on you."

He paused. "I don't like firing people, you know. And I've fired people all across the continental United States."

"You did a good job with this company," Tom said, aware the man was broadcasting loneliness on all known frequencies. Tom was also aware that, close to a panic state over money, he was comforting a man without a money worry in the world.

"The free market sucks but is better than the alternatives," the man replied.

Tom said, "People should realize how much harm we're doing to our souls."

"Should, agreed. But won't happen. The free market makes people heartless. Has to, in order to function properly. Go to any high-demographic zip code, knock on any door. The people there, even the PC ones who contribute to NPR and want to save the manatee, in their hearts all that really matters to them is they are on top. They'll pay five hundred dollars a night for a resort room without blinking, and at the same time expect the workers at the child-care centers where they leave their children to act grateful for six-fifty an hour. The folks who claim a social conscience and have it made, do they give money away? They put additions on their houses, is what they do."

The man sealed a box with packing tape and affixed a FedEx waybill. He jotted a cell number on an elegant business card, made of expensive stock, on which was printed only his name. He handed the card to Tom, saying, "I'll head to Cambridge next week and check out biotech start-ups spinning off from MIT. Life-extension drugs are a hot play. Americans complain nonstop about their lives, and would spend anything to prolong them. The soup is terrible and such small portions, eh? If I hear of any start-ups that need a good front man, I'll let you know."

Tom waited alone until a courier service came to pick up the boxes. The soup is terrible and such small portions—that old Vaudeville line could sum what it means to face life.

The empty office, a week before buzzing with people and hopes, suggested a stage that had been struck following the final performance of a show. As Tom was departing, a team of illegal immigrants arrived: they would work through the wee hours cleaning so the office space could be shown to potential customers in the morning. The cleaners were happy with midnight work, as this paid double-time. Some had taken great risks crossing a desert to arrive in a country where there was so much going on, offices needed to be vacated in the middle of the night. Tom drove to an extended-stay hotel that he'd need to leave in the morning.

Chapter 5

November 2008

Record decline in housing prices.
U.S. motor vehicle production: 8.7 million.
Economy contracts for third consecutive quarter.

The townhouse was nice, adequate certainly, though Margo found it unsettling to have walls that were shared with someone else. Whose were the walls?

As a college student, then as a footloose bachelorette, then in the place with Tom in Lincoln Park, she'd not only wanted her own home but come to view the detached home, framed by driveway and lawn, as symbolic of the reestablishment of the norm she knew in girlhood. Her first awareness of the world came in a house separate from other houses. When Margo became the mother of a new family of her creation, she desired the same equation of house-equals-home.

They were able to afford the rent for the second

floor, so no sound of walking on the ceiling. And on the second floor, she heard less of the slamming. Car doors slammed throughout the townhouse complex at all hours. Why is it people think a car door must be slammed to close? Initially, Margo sought a logical explanation. Perhaps people arriving at two A.M., rather than close their car doors quietly in consideration of others, slammed them as a way of announcing they'd worked extra-long, or been out partying, or felt angry that others slept while they weren't yet home. Eventually she realized people slam car doors for this reason: because they have brains the size of acorns.

Being on the second floor reduced the parking-area sounds but meant no deck or patio. Margo couldn't walk outside and sit reading the newspaper. There was no yard, no place of their own to toss a ball or light off smuggled fireworks on the Fourth of July. The yard and deck were a small loss—no one needs a yard. But they'd had a fabulous house and now had only an adequate townhouse. The family was going in the wrong direction.

The girls sensed there was something not right about the sudden decision to sell the sort of house they assumed every girl lived in, except for the kind of children one hears about on television. Margo and

Tom told them the family was moving in order to live closer to their new school. The girls did not want a new school. It wasn't so much that they grasped the distinction between leaving private education for public. Rather, it was that they were deep into the social scene at Pinnacle Ácademy, and just getting good. Navigating that school's complex cartography of tween and teen social markers was, so far, the biggest accomplishment in life for Caroline and Megan.

Any adult would have known immediately the real cause of the move was money. But neither of the girls ever asked about the family situation with money, a topic children from all backgrounds tend to view as either distant and unimportant or very, very scary.

Before the move, Margo overheard her daughters whispering about whether Mom and Dad were getting divorced. She and Tom became excessively sunny, like actors in a dish-detergent commercial. Divorce was the nighttime dread of many kids at Pinnacle. The children from divorces were put in the middle of arguments they had nothing to do with, employed as pressure points. They could side with one parent and be scorned as disloyal by the other, or side with neither and be found insufficiently loving by both. Not a lot of attractive options there from the children's standpoint. A few at the school overcompensated by boasting about how really great it was their parents finally split up.

"The girls' room is lovely," Lillian said. She had come over to assist in the latter phase of moving in—hanging pictures on walls, setting out tchotchkes.

"There was a fight about giving up their own rooms," Margo said, slightly weary. "A fight about who got which bed. A fight about sharing a computer instead of one for each of them. A fight about—well, I could save time by telling you what there wasn't a fight about."

"They'll get used to the new situation."

"Tell them in twenty years when they will listen."

Lillian said, "How I wish I'd had a sister to share my room with."

Often children are told that bad things—divorces, sudden moves, sports defeats, embarrassments around friends—are happening for their own good. "It's a blessing in disguise," among the hackneyed comments in the human phrase book, is like saying, "This tornado is a sunny day in disguise." Margo had always disliked "It's a blessing in disguise" and all variants, such as

"God works in mysterious ways," a phrase often heard in sermons but not encountered in scripture.

In scripture, God is not mysterious, except as regards origin: there are specific, clearly enunciated divine ends, coupled to God's frustration in achieving them. To Margo, most of life's frustrations and wrong turns were bad luck or just really sucked—she was more comfortable telling the girls "This really sucks" than announcing a blessing in disguise. But she failed in being honest with them about the move, though knew she should have been. Nothing mysterious there.

At least, Margo could tell herself, she never used the alibi "Everything happens for a reason." People said to each other "Everything happens for a reason" in order to palliate grief. But if everything happens for a reason, the world is in even worse shape than feared.

The procession of delivery trucks did not arrive at the townhouse, as had been the case at their home. But there was a plastic package on the table, ripped by a zipper line, with a pair of inexpensive casual pants for Tom—the kind that someone on the sales floor of a hardware store would wear. "Had to exchange the last one, he needs a larger waistline," Margo said. "Most places are so good now about returns. Tom has this theory that he should only own two pairs of slacks, both from Bean's or Lands' End. Each time one wears out, he would send it back, insisting on a replacement, and wear the other till the new one came. Never have to pay for slacks again."

Lillian remembered something she'd been told at a party, information that, at the time, seemed fantastical to her, given her naïveté about shopping culture: "I've heard of women who purchase stunning jewelry from Tiffany or thousand-dollar party dresses, wear them to an event where everyone goes ooh and ahh, then the next day return them for a refund, claiming dissatisfaction."

Margo said, "Really!" She left out that she had done this. Though the claim of dissatisfaction was easy enough to believe.

"I was watching cable news," Lillian said. "Today's scandal is the governor having affairs. With persons of the opposite gender. At least there's a refreshing change of pace."

"How does anyone have time for affairs?" Margo asked. In her twenties, she wanted romance to fill her every available hour. Now she had no available hours. "My day is broken down into ten-minute intervals of work, driving and chores. Who has a period in the afternoon that isn't already accounted for? When does this governor find time to seduce?"

"I suspect politicians don't seduce," Lillian said. "Presumably it's all arranged by the staff."

"Still." Margo said this in the way the word "still" can be converted via inflection into a sentence. "If someone arranged to have Will Smith waiting for me in a hotel room, my first words would be, 'This needs to be quick.'"

"Cable showed the governor giving the mandatory tearful speech, stalwart wife by his side. Let's hope she has a percentage of the book rights," Lillian said.

"Maybe she set her own husband up with an intern so she could get a divorce and a movie sale all in the same package. That would prove this really is the twenty-first century."

They laughed. Margo said, "Before Tom gets home—you seem all right, are you all right?"

"Why wouldn't I be?"

"I mean, hasn't it been five years?"

"Five exactly," Lillian said. "I'm touched you would remember the date."

Sheepish, Margo indicated her smart phone. "I put the date in here," she explained. Then stopped and said, "Should I not have placed something so personal and private in an electronic device?" The smart phone was efficient but callous. Diaries and notebooks are inefficient, but seem warm to the touch.

"I had a difficult time last night, knowing today would be five years," Lillian said. "Then when I woke up I felt fine. Is it wrong for me to feel fine?"

Margo felt nothing about her friend could ever be wrong. That Lillian was fine on the morning that marked the fifth anniversary of Madeline's death seemed a sign her period of grief was ending, assuming one could ever stop grieving a child's death.

"I think it's good that you feel fine, this is what Madeleine would want," Margo said. Grief counselors often tell relatives or survivors that the dead would want them to be happy. This may be hollow sentiment, but it's not exactly as if grief counselors have a huge toolkit at their disposal. "Do you want to talk about her?"

"No," Lillian replied. "What I want is to change the subject."

Since Margo had mentioned her cell phone, Lillian supposed she might know something about computers, and asked her how to back up hard drives. Lillian had been working for a decade on a history of village art in Carpathian Ruthenia. Her manuscript and all her notes were on disk—if a passing comet caused electricity to stop flowing, the entire project would vanish. She'd chosen Carpathian Ruthenia because she believed it the sole period no art historian had done. Lillian lived in terror of coming across a university-house publication catalog listing an upcoming title like *Representationalism Among the Proto-Magyars: Volume One.*

Margo told her any one of her students—anyone under age twenty-five—could answer any question about electronics. Then Margo wondered aloud when Tom would be home, saying indistinctly that in his new job Tom did not control his hours.

The two women spent some time arranging furniture to try to make the place seem larger. Tom and Margo had put a lot into storage, finding themselves having to pay for not being able to use something. Selling off furniture they couldn't fit into the town-home did not make financial sense. If Craigslist and the classifieds were any guide, the Vermont cherry armoire Margo spent five thousand dollars on only a few years before—a superb piece—might fetch five hundred dollars now, and that was assuming a buyer could be found. They owned a mahogany dining-room set, a dozen chairs and a table suitable for King Arthur and his knights. Margo wanted big, for the dinner parties she loved to throw. The table did not fit in the townhome dining room, and she couldn't let it go for a fraction of what it cost. So the table was in storage, along with six of the chairs. At least they still had a dining room. Some of the townhomes in their complex did not, only a breakfast nook. How could one live without a dining room?

Margo thought about the dreary day she and Tom drove up to the place whose sign announced, SELF-STORAGE. She told Tom that only in America do businesses offer storage of the self, and chuckled at her own joke. Soon she realized the joke was not funny—everyone she glimpsed arriving at or departing from the self-storage facility appeared to be fairly far along into some phase of sadness or personal failure.

Margo heard a car door outside and then the chirp-chirp of the alarm activating, the modern car being better protected than the modern person. Tom entered, carrying plastic-handle bags with the 7-Eleven logo. He was dressed in a sales-floor clerk's vest of Restoration Hardware, and wore on his belt a circular clip containing many keys on a retractable lanyard.

Margo looked at the bags in a disapproving manner. "The grocery store is cheaper," she said. Yet she
should have gone out to pick up a few things—it had
been inconsiderate of her to expect Tom to stop on
his way home.

"Sorry, I'm just tired," Tom said. "At the grocery
store you park like a mile from the door then the inside is so big, you wander. At the new Safeway they
have an aisle for domestic water and another entire
aisle for imported water. I'm too tired for such a big
place after a day on my feet. Seven-Eleven is tempt-
ing: just pull up, grab it, get out. They practically push
you out. You don't think about paying too much."

"'Too much' is a matter of point of view," Lillian
said. "Convenience has a cost, like any other commod-
ity or service. Everything comes with a price."

In the economics department at her college, statements such as that were not intended to be harsh, merely
analytical: *Students, in this class we will discuss the scarcity concept that underlines neoclassical economics. In order
for the market to allocate resources efficiently, everything
must come with a price. . . .*"

Even in a utopia, the doctors would earn more than
the cabdrivers and command more purchasing power.

It is not hard to imagine a society both utopian yet having price-allocation via scarcity, plus significant inequality. Suppose the minimum annual income were $100,000—paid even to janitors and hotel maids—while the maximum annual income rose in steps, based on job value, to $500,000. There would be significant inequality in such a society, and also plenty of incentive to become a surgeon or inventor or pilot, to earn the maximum. The incentive would ensure productivity while rewarding talent, keeping society vibrant. Yet there would be no poverty nor any extreme wealth. Wouldn't this be utopian? But all that is college talk. For most people, the knowledge that "everything comes with a price" is a lifelong curse.

Tom put the bags on the counter—eggs, bread, American cheese slices, beer, a discount brand of ground coffee that cost more in 7-Eleven than premium whole bean in a grocery store. The bread was a new variety, whole-wheat white, which sounded a bit like low-fat bacon. The label proclaimed the bread to be Soft 'N' Hearty and declared the product possessed Fresh Baked Taste. Not that the bread was fresh baked; rather, it had fresh-baked taste. Perhaps there was no meaningful difference between being fresh and tasting fresh. Products on grocers' shelves now say things like MADE FROM REAL POTATOES. And "real potatoes" differ from "potatoes" . . . how, exactly?

Tom felt self-conscious about shopping at 7-Eleven and paying the price of convenience. "Now I notice the people who frequent convenience stores," he said. "They arrive in brand-new monster-sized pickup trucks with all the options; that can't have been a smart decision. People who should not be blowing five bucks on a travel-sized laundry detergent, they should be buying the jumbo size in a regular store and getting thirty washes for the same price. But they're too disorganized to shop properly, or to think more than a couple loads of laundry ahead. The kind of petty blunders they make at the 7-Eleven symbolize the other decisions that hold them back in life, like impulse marriages or runaway credit-card debt. And the store itself—the marketing, it's designed to cause you to make petty blunders."

"I can see stopping at a 7-Eleven if you need to pick up milk or a candy bar," Lillian said. "Otherwise one does not belong in such places."

"I feel I do now, somehow," Tom said.

Margo was talking on her cell to Caroline, who was at a birthday party; Megan was at a different birthday party, on the opposite end of the county. Often Margo talked to her girls for longer periods by phone than when they were in the same room.

"I'm trying to pay for things like groceries with cash; it's more disciplined than using a card," Tom told Lillian. "There is too much credit-card debt!" He said this too strongly for a casual conversation. "Even these smooth-looking professional couples who come into the store, they want home Jacuzzis or a built-in gas fireplace on time. I take their credit statements. They have five cards maxed out and they're looking for fresh credit. Usually they get it."

Margo had finished talking to Caroline and listened to the last few statements. "People make mistakes with money because it's so easy to," she supposed. "Imagine if you could have all the sex you wanted right now, delivered with a friendly smile, and you just had to sign a piece of paper acknowledging you were warned there would be complications later."

"I'd sign!" Lillian said brightly.

"Credit cards are like that," Margo said. "You can have the tennis bracelet or the Rolex right now, tonight, and being able to buy it feels like an achievement. Later when the bill arrives you think it's somehow unfair you have to pay, because you've already lost interest in whatever you bought." Margo had noticed the girls talked with keen anticipation about material things they wanted—types of phones, brands of clothes. Once the desired item was obtained, they lost interest and began speaking of the next thing wished for.

"My theory," Lillian said, "is that people buy what they can't afford because subconsciously they believe they will die anyway before the debts add up." Tom shot her a look, though neither woman noticed.

Margo had enjoyed the years in which Tom's rising income allowed her to purchase that which she didn't need. But she was also aware that simply buying what strikes one's fancy, without any long-term plan for lean times, is not wise for a family, let alone a nation.

"If buying on debt gets you what you want, many people don't think beyond that," she said. "Walk into a showroom and sign some forms, they give you a bedroom set. The consequences are down the road." To buy without seeming to pay by using credit, especially gimmick debts like nothing down or no payments till next year, was, Margo thought, like reverting to the habits of a child. You'd ask your parents for something and they would give it to you. There was no price to be paid later, no consequences, no sense that the parents faced money limits . . . the child's challenge was simply to twist Mom's and Dad's arms until they provided what was wanted. The nation had grown childish, she thought—interest groups saw their challenge as twisting congressional arms until their special favor was provided, without discussing the debt cost or consequences. For children to think that way was human nature. For the leaders of a country to think that way was frightening.

Lillian asked, "You turned the Lexus back in to the dealer, didn't you?" She had noticed the car gone from the townhouse driveway.

"The lease was up soon, and the Hyundai has a better warranty," Margo replied, in the same voice she once used when declaring that she didn't really want the lead in her high-school senior play. It was a dumb play. It was a dumb Lexus.

Lillian said something about ordering out dinner. Tom didn't want to hear that. They'd decided to eliminate restaurant food; it was spooky how easily a delivered Chinese dinner turned out to be sixty dollars. Before he could say anything, Lillian volunteered to go out to pick up food and some wine. Tom grimaced and reached for his wallet; Lillian waved her hand, saying she would treat. Tom felt embarrassed.

"I'm going to fix this," he told Margo after Lillian

left. "I've got a plan and it works one way or the other. One way or the other."

Lately Tom had been making enigmatic references to having a plan. Margo found this discomforting, as he would not explain. She began to ask him again but Tom said, "I have to open tomorrow. I need to be there at five A.M. to let the stockers in. That means I have to be in the shower at four A.M. If I don't disarm the security at precisely five A.M., proving I was there, I don't get to work the next extra shift."

Margo protested, "Tomorrow is Sunday!"

She knew if he needed to report to the store that early, inevitably Tom would wolf down dinner and be asleep at nine. And who wants to be driving to work in the dark on a Sunday morning?

"It's only a matter of time till the store goes twenty-four hours," Tom said. "The new globalized economic model is that whenever any part of the world is working, every part ought to be working." First capitalism was going to make everyone equally impoverished. Then communism was going to make everyone equally miserable. Now global economics will make everyone equally sleep-deprived.

"Try to be careful about giving hints about our situation in front of Lillian," Margo said. "She doesn't know how bad it is. I don't want her to find out you have to get up before sunrise on Sunday to go to a hardware store."

"A *furnishings* store," Tom said, enjoying being snide. "They coach us to avoid the word 'hardware.' We sell faucets, but they are not hardware. They are *home solutions.*" Margo laughed and kissed him and pressed her crotch against his. He did not press back.

Margo needed some lovin' and she also needed oxytocin, though she did not know that detail of biochemistry. The intense pleasure of orgasm lasts thirty seconds; oxytocin, released during sexual arousal, dwells in the body for about a week, causing a feeling of contentedness. Married people and long-term couples always get along better if they've had sex recently—because of the pleasure, sure, but also because a contentedness hormone is flowing. Long-term human relationships involve a lot of stress that the single person does not experience. One of the compensations is the warm, empathetic sensations that come in the aftermath of sex. If you have a regular partner, you experience the warm feeling regularly. Probably this had something to do with our distant ancestors forming the antecedents of family groups.

Seeming exhausted, Tom began to speak. "Today

a man comes in, sixty maybe. I know someday I'll say sixty is the new forty. He's got the lemon tart in tow, half his age. The kind who's too thin, too much eye shadow, can hardly balance her heels are so high, looks hot from a distance but the closer she gets the less good she looks. She's talking on the cell the entire time and also chewing gum, doesn't even speak to me, just points at things. I show him the top-of-the-line SubZero refrigerator, forty-nine-inch doors, six thousand dollars. He says, 'Don't you have anything nicer?' I show him the latest camelback sofas—four thousand for a freaking sofa—he says, 'Don't you have anything more impressive?' Tells me he just got the kind of wine cooler that you have to reinforce the floor for. I show him countertops, tell him what country the various classes of granite come from. He wants to know specifically which quarry—only wants granite from a quarry that has been in continuous use since Roman days. The lemon tart read about that in an airline magazine. At least she can read.

"Three hours I spent with this couple. I write them for a seventy-thousand-dollar kitchen makeover, including lapis trim and granite backsplash. Would have been my best commission. He says they have to go out for a drink to think about it. Hour later they come back, I don't see them walk in. They sign the deal, exactly the deal I wrote, with another salesman. Didn't ask for me. And this asshole, what does he do for a living? Bonds broker. So he knows about commissions."

"Sounds like you had a bad day."

"We needed that commission."

"There will be other rich twits." She tried to change his focus by fiddling with his shirt buttons and licking her lips. There was nothing in life that brought Tom more happiness than her tongue.

"The steering pump on the Taurus is shot, the clothes dryer doesn't make hot air," Tom said, not noticing. "Those right there will knock out a week's pay."

"Something will happen to change our luck."

"We were close to being rich. Now I work a sales floor. It's supposed to be hard to climb the economic ladder. But sliding backward isn't supposed to happen."

"The big companies will start hiring again," Margo said. "You'll end up in management. Somewhere important, at the kind of company that doesn't even need a name, just initials."

"It's been months since the last headhunter called."

Since Tom now had no office, Margo heard him as

he sat at the kitchen table, placing calls, asking if companies wanted his résumé, laboring to sound upbeat and confident. He was trying to seem as though he were sorting through a stack of offers. If they know you're actually sitting at a kitchen table, they're not interested. It was excruciating for Margo to hear her husband begging for work.

Tom looked at Margo softly and embraced her, saying, "At least I have a wife who looks better the closer you get."

"Do you think we have time before Lillian gets back?" Margo asked. Tom shook his head no. They kissed—that was some consolation.

"Don't worry, babe," she said. "The world screws everybody. The answer to the great cosmic question of why we are here is that we are here to be screwed." Philosophers and theologians have pondered for centuries why we are here. In recent decades cosmologists have joined the discourse, as indications of the anthropocentric character of the universe increasingly suggest that some form, at least, of life was anticipated. Margo felt that regardless of the value of the fine-structure constant or other sorts of issues debated by physicists, humanity had to exist so the universe could have a victim. If there were no intelligent life, then no one could be miserable, and this outcome was simply impermissible under natural law.

"There must be higher purpose," Tom said. "Something led me to you."

They kissed anew, then parted with a start on the sound of a car door slamming loudly outside, though this turned out not to be Lillian.

"I went to meet Caroline's guidance counselor today," Margo said. "The high school—it's—it's nice."

"It's not nice?" Obviously that was what she meant.

"I had never been inside a school that needs paint."

"The SAT averages are okay and the college-attendance rate is okay. Isn't that all that matters?"

"I know it was snobby to send them to private school. But that ensured a good peer group. The new school has a lot of kids from broken families, troubled situations."

Initially Margo had thought it would be good for the girls to attend a public school where they would meet children of different backgrounds. She hadn't thought through that this meant teens who never studied, whose parents were absent, who came from a milieu of failure and subconsciously assumed failure would be their lot. High-school students learn as much from their families and peer groups as from teachers.

Reflecting this, studies show that stability in the home is a better predictor of educational success than IQ, household income, race or any other factor. Her girls were dropped into an environment of children from unstable homes, something the U.S. economy was now producing with the same fervor it once produced Oldsmobiles.

Tom knew Margo's unease about the school was not a reflection on him, but he took it that way regardless. "To get kids into the good public schools, you must be able to afford a place within the boundaries," he said.

Officially public-school systems are equal to all, but the For Sale sign on the lawn now serves the function segregation once did. The high-quality public schools are open only to those who live within their boundaries—and housing within those boundaries costs more than housing within the boundaries of weak public-school systems. Credit histories and down payments sift who gets into good public schools and who doesn't: and though the current system was not intended to cause racial divisions, it operates as if it were. Margo and Tom had always known that property values had become the new gatekeepers of schools.

But they'd been exempt from this problem before. Now they had to deal with it.

"Tom, if the girls aren't admitted to an Ivy or Stanford or Bowdoin, I won't be able to take it."

"Everything is going to be fine."

"I want the University of Chicago bumper sticker. That is not pettiness—sending our children on to something better should be one of life's rewards. Put the bumper sticker on a Hyundai, fine. Just give me the University of Chicago bumper sticker."

"My card was rejected today," Tom said. There was no good moment to tell her.

Instinctively, Margo was fearful. "What card?"

"The bank card. I stopped at an ATM for cash. Wouldn't give any. I went to another, in case the machine was the problem. The same."

"Our bank account is empty?"

"Every time I turn around I'm writing a check or handing someone a twenty."

"*Empty?*"

"Work hard like we have—when you press the button, money is supposed to come out."

"This must be a mistake," Margo said. "I'll go to the bank and talk to the manager." She realized she

had not spoken to a bank manager in at least a decade—
they did everything electronically. Margo couldn't
swear there even still were bank lobbies with well-
dressed personnel waiting to receive customers at desks.

"Work and spend, that's the valor of our era," Tom
said, without enough emotion to be disconsolate. "If
you get good grades then work hard and swallow your
thoughts at the right times, when you push the button, money comes out." This was the bargain most
people of Tom and Margo's generation made, to sur-
render some larger fulfillment in return for ordering
whatever they want in restaurants. Tom paused, then
repeated: "When you push the button, money must
come out!"

"This is going to be okay, babe."

"Some checks I wrote are going to bounce."

"Bounced checks!" Margo shivered; the words
made her feel like a swindler. "The girls must not find
this out," she said.

"The rich bounce checks all the time," Tom said.
"They're too big to fail. Us—we are just the right size
to fail."

"'Fail'? What do you mean, fail?" Margo had never
heard Tom speak so pessimistically.

"One way or the other this ends with the family

back on top and the girls having everything again," he said, trying to sound assured. "One way or the other. I've already laid everything out."

"What do you mean, 'ends'?"

Chapter 6

March 2009

Dow Jones Index: 6,700.

U.S. motor vehicle production: 5.7 million.

Unemployment: 9 percent.

Because management and labor refused to speak to each other, the city convention center needed facilitators—or Facilitators, as their duty descriptions read. The capital letter was the main perk of the job.

Labor costs were dragging the center down: union carpenters and helpers who set up and then struck the floor exhibits and breakout rooms received the same wage whether they worked or sat, and for every worker actually present there was a no-show ghost employee drawing wages partly rebated to a local crime boss. The labor contracts were all political, with twice as much money siphoned off by featherbedding and kickbacks as was invested in actual convention-center activity.

Management was no rose either. The convention center had an executive suite where dozens of senior-grade managers received lavish salaries for doing nothing—if they arrived in the morning at all, since the politically connected ones skipped work for days or weeks at a time without anything being said. Those senior-grade managers who deigned to report rarely emerged from the executive area. Instead they passed orders to the Facilitators, generally by text message to avoid personal interaction or the faintest appearance of effort.

Tom, now a Facilitator, had to take a deep breath each time he approached a steward. Twenty carpenters and their helpers could be sitting all morning idle and the steward would say that moving a table was completely impossible.

The exhibitors who paid the center's exorbitant fees were forbidden to speak to labor and were never able to find anyone in management, so they dealt almost entirely with Facilitators, who could speak to stewards, though never to workers. And no matter what the request was, from the stewards the answer always was no.

Labor floated along demanding overtime and filing grievances, oblivious to the center's poor reputation and declining bookings. Management floated along doing nothing of value other than stroking the right contacts at City Hall. Caught between the two, Facilitators were supposed to make the convention center function. To free up more money for featherbedding and bribes, the year before, the career Facilitators—the institutional memory, the people who actually knew what they were doing—had been laid off. Rather, been "excessed," as their disclaimer-covered dismissal notices said. Now Facilitators were hired as temp employees with no benefits or rights, as well as no experience or knowledge. This was another factor in the center's decline. But no one in the executive suite or union leadership cared about that in the slightest, as long as there was public money to steal from.

All told, it was a pretty modern American situation. Just add borrowing!

The city council knew about how bad the situation was at the convention center, but rather than act—any plan of action would have entailed crossing an interest group—tried to postpone the day of reckoning by selling municipal bonds against future revenues. This allowed the convention center to fall further and further into debt, but also kept up the flow of patronage jobs and kickbacks. So many revenue bonds were in circulation that the city had, in effect, sold the convention center's potential income several times over. All that mattered to investors was the bond yield, which could be covered by selling additional bonds—a Ponzi arrangement not unlike Washington selling more Treasury bills to cover deficits caused by runaway spending. The convention-center bonds were tax-exempt, which was appealing to investors while hurting the civic tax base. Shifting fiscal harm into the future in return for a cookie jar today was the political magic formula of the moment. City council members knew they'd be retired, with handsome bank accounts, by the time the bills for this funny business came due. Besides, why not follow the example set by the nation's capital? A mere city government could only gaze in admiration at the scale of stealing and squandering in Washington.

There was a purity of purpose to the union. Its leaders single-mindedly pursued a vision of putting any firm or government agency their local worked for into receivership, at which point the union members would be fortunate to find jobs that paid a third of the wage they currently complained so much about. The convention-center executives, for their parts, were amateurs compared to Fortune 500 executives. Convention center executives were mismanaging tens of millions— Fortune 500 executives mismanaged billions.

Restoration Hardware "furloughed" Tom—at least it didn't "excess" him—saying he would be called back as soon as sales picked up when the Great Recession ended. At least retail would always require people. When manufacturing picked up again, most workers would never be called back, since automation was causing manufacturing productivity to rise fast. An auto plant built today needs a tenth the workforce of a plant of the same capacity built in the 1950s, and makes better cars that are safer and last longer. Unless you propose to ban advances in technology and engineering—and its unclear how that might be accomplished, even if you were so inclined—the next generation of auto plants and other factories will need even fewer workers.

Some economists thought that what seemed to the political and media elite like a 2008 financial freeze that caused rising unemployment was actually two unrelated events in progress simultaneously. The 2008 financial freeze was real enough, but the unemployment rise would have happened regardless, because automation technology was the primary influence. Six million American manufacturing jobs had been lost since 1980. But factory jobs weren't fleeing to China, as pundits and antiglobalists claimed: China lost 28 million manufacturing jobs in the same period, even with go-go growth. And American manufacturing was not in decline, as the editorial pages kept saying: U.S. manufacturing output hit records, even for steel, throughout the first decade of the twenty-first century. It's just that ever more stuff was produced by ever fewer workers. Globally the picture was the same. Soon there wouldn't be any nation on Earth, including in Asia, with a jobs base anchored in manufacturing.

The political world was oblivious to this, and kept throwing borrowed money at subsidized manufacturing that generates a small number of extremely expensive jobs that technology soon wipes out anyway. Freeing the human family from factory labor is, long-term, an advance, just as was freeing the human family from subsistence agriculture. Short-term, this transition was making a mess of Western economies, and all the political class could think of was to use the situation as a rationalization for handing more favors to campaign donors.

After being laid off from hardware sales, Tom saw an online ad for what seemed like white-collar positions at the convention center. Perhaps a hundred men and women started queuing up at dawn for interviews for a few temporary positions—men in expensive suits and women who'd taken the subway there wearing sneakers but with elegant pumps in their bags. Each held briefcases stuffed with résumés and letters of recommendation. Then there were no interviews. The first five in the line simply were hired and the rest sent away without being spoken to. Tom had arrived while it was still dark, and so was hired.

"Nobody's set up the booth for Bayliner," Tom told a steward. "That was supposed to be completed two days ago. The boat show opens tomorrow."

"Yesterday we moved a thousand chairs; that's all I can manage with just forty men," the steward said. "You want a faster pace, increase hiring." He smoked indoors, although the center was no-smoking.

"A dozen high-school kids could have moved those chairs and done it in half the time," Tom said. "The booths should be ready. The customers should get what they pay for."

"You are creating an unwelcoming workplace environment," the steward replied, wheeled, and walked away.

The steward was stalling until three P.M., when his

crew could begin to collect overtime. Tom had to go mollify Bayliner once again. Three tractor-trailer trucks hauling the company's cuddies and cabin cruisers were parked outside the center, waiting for the retractable wall to open so the cargo could be brought in. The stewards kept saying it was "unsafe" to open the wall unless workers got United Nations Day as a paid holiday.

The annual boat show was going ahead despite the economy, $150,000 cabin cruisers everywhere you looked. This year's star was a $2 million Dominator 64 with three cabins, three heads, a bunk area for crew members and a gas grill for seagoing cookouts. Recreational boats seemed a strange market sector to be promoting at the trough of a recession. But if the boat show were canceled because of the economy, that wouldn't send much of a message. The annual show provided two weeks of work for hundreds of people, including emcees, ushers and models who lounged in swimsuits at the exhibits; bikini models put men in the mood to spend. Almost all fancy boats are purchased by men. Something about the combination of engineering, impracticality, one-upmanship and babe-appeal fantasy made the luxury boat a particularly male space.

Just two generations ago, many families didn't own a car. Now America boasted 14 million registered private recreational boats, many with mast radar.

Tom went to find the woman in charge of the Bayliner exhibit. He knew she'd be steamed; she had to hire rent-a-cops to sit outside overnight with her fancy boats that weren't being allowed in. He'd already gotten an earful from her about how nothing like this ever happened at the Fort Lauderdale or San Diego shows and her firm wouldn't be back. Tom really needed to placate her.

The Facilitator contracts were show-to-show, which meant being ritually fired as each show concluded. Getting fired every couple of weeks—what could be more current? Tom needed the Bayliner woman to say something nice about him so he'd be rehired for the hunting convention coming up the following month. That was expected to be a media event: the sponsors were going to haul in soil and trees, let some deer loose in an enclosure and raffle off the chance to shoot them. If there were too many complaints from the current exhibitors, the politically protected types in the executive suite were sure to blame the Facilitators and bring in new staff who would make learning-experience errors, then be fired.

Should I call her by her first name? Tom was thinking as he looked for the Bayliner woman. His social class was the same as hers. An unskilled worker would be expected to address her by her last name, while someone who is white-collar would speak less formally. The way a person announces another name's may cue social class; addressing a physician as "Bob" instead of "Dr. Martindale" conveys your status as roughly the same as his. Tom wondered whether calling the Bayliner woman Amanda would communicate in a single word, *I, too, was once an executive on Easy Street, and you could end up like me amazingly fast.* Then she would say something nice about him rather than complain.

But what were the odds that, under any circumstances, a contemporary American would pass on the chance to complain?

There were boxes, pieces of sets and half-completed audiovisual gear in the Bayliner exhibit area. But no Amanda and, sadly for Tom, no models previewing their bikinis. There was one man working alone, whom Tom did not recognize. The man was lying on his back, assembling some stage pieces. He didn't wear one of the CIA-style photo-and-bar-code IDs found on convention-center personnel.

"Who are you?" Tom asked simply.

The man looked around. "She told me not to let anyone see me," he said.

He wasn't trying to take anything—rather, was putting things together. As far as Tom knew, felonious assembly is not a crime.

"Did the Bayliner woman hire you?"

"Yeah. Temp agency sent me and a couple other guys to babysit her fancy boats last night. Gave us these." He indicated a navy windbreaker, which said EVENT STAFF in big yellow letters on the back. It was designed to resemble an FBI field windbreaker, as if handing these to untrained temps turned them into a security force to be feared. Maybe criminals are afraid of the words "Event Staff."

So the Bayliner woman hadn't hired rent-a-cops as she claimed—that did sound pricey. Rather, she brought in minimum-wage guys armed with windbreakers. Tom wondered if she would send the convention center a false invoice claiming a major expense for rent-a-cops.

"When she showed up this morning, she offered me a hundred bucks to assemble this stage and wire the loudspeakers," the man continued. "She was going off about I shouldn't let anyone see what I was doing. Why does she care if anybody sees?"

Exhibitors weren't allowed to bring in their own laborers; everything had to go through channels. There would be a huge dustup if this was noticed. Hours would be spent yelling about a matter that could have been resolved in minutes, if the people in the unaccountable positions weren't in need of something to get upset about.

"I'll help you," Tom said. He grabbed some tools. When Tom had to lean all the way forward to lift a heavy part, compressing his stomach and chest, for a moment he felt without breath.

"Thanks, pal. You're all right. Kevin."

"Tom."

Kevin Parquet hadn't done a masterful job with his life. In youth leagues, then in high school, he had been a basketball and baseball star, his parents filling much of a den with sports trophies he'd won by age fifteen. Everyone wanted to be his friend. Homework, studying—if you're good, the college will just change your grades, that's what somebody told him at a basketball camp. He had been five-foot-ten at age ten but was still five-foot-ten at age eighteen. Early-maturity boys grow up thinking they will be sports stars, but late-maturity boys dominate the top levels of athletics. Nobody tells that to the early-maturity boys, who enjoy a few young years living an illusion of fame to come, and then, if they never studied in high school, can't get regular admission to college.

"Has he started shaving yet?" is one of the first questions college recruiters ask about teen male prospects. The answer they want to hear is no; that means late maturity, more size and more strength on the way. The equation is different for teen female athletes, since girls develop physically so much faster than boys. At a high-school freshman dance, half the girls will look like they belong in porn videos, while half the boys will look like they should be home playing with LEGOs. The boys who are baby-faced are the ones who will have Greek-god physiques in their early twenties. Kevin started shaving at age fourteen. He was excited, thinking it meant he had loads of testosterone; actually it was a bad sign about his recruiting chances. As a senior he received no college offers, and his GPA made even community college a dicey proposition.

His father had a small contracting firm that replaced roofs on houses. Kevin worked there for a few years, but when his father died, the company folded— the men who went up on the roofs would listen to Kevin's father, but not to him. Speeding and DUI tickets started Kevin on a cycle of decline: soon a big chunk of his sporadic income went to fines and sky-high auto insurance. Sometimes people become mired in the lower class because much of what they earn arrives already spoken for, to be spent on past mistakes.

Kevin's first wife fell ill and died young, like women did in nineteenth-century novels. Don't assume this does not happen anymore. Kevin soon married again, looking to put his life back on course. But it was an impulse union to a woman he barely knew, who got excited when she heard Kevin's father had owned a company, and from this assumed Kevin had money hidden somewhere. The second wife left for another man and filed a false charge of battery against Kevin, believing that would force Kevin to give her hush money to drop the accusation. His ex began calling him in the middle of the night, drunk, demanding to know where her "settlement" was. Kevin got the impression the ex and her new beau spent a lot of time strategizing about how to wring money from him.

Things went downhill from there: odd jobs, disturbing the peace. His previous night's work baby-sitting boats, and now the cash for setting up the exhibit, would put nearly two hundred dollars in

Kevin's pocket, the most that had been there in some time. It would all be gone by midnight.

Tom realized there was alcohol on Kevin's breath, though it was midmorning. Close-up, he could see aging lines on Kevin's face—creases that made his skin appear to be a kind of fabric, though he was only in his late thirties. People who went to good colleges and got good jobs groused all the time about stress but seemed to age less than those who didn't. This seemed likely to continue to be the case as long as the good jobs lasted, anyway.

Chapter 7

June 2009

General Motors enters bankruptcy.
35,000-year-old flute unearthed in a Swabian cave.
National debt: $12 trillion.

Seated at the apartment's kitchen table, Margo felt confined. The table was too big for the available area: to sit she had to push it away then pull it back, repeating the process to stand. She had papers spread in front of her, the majority of them bills and invoices. The cell phone was open, set to speaker, playing excruciating elevator music: a saccharine version of "She Loves Me" flowed into a worse orchestral of "Some Enchanted Evening." Margo was speaking into the landline phone while listening for something on the cell phone:

"Then the guidance counselor told me Caroline has not turned in homework for a month. She was watching the mailbox for the warning letter; she ripped it up. I'm at my wit's end, how will she get into college? She will be up against these brainiac kids with great SATs and awards for attending oboe recitals in Copenhagen. She'll never get into a good college with a D on her transcript. And her only activity is the pop-star-impersonators club."

The cell phone made an electronic squelch. Margo said into the regular phone, "Damn, I was just disconnected on the other line. Hold on a second while I redial."

The townhouse, lost with disturbing speed, seemed a dim memory though they'd left only two months before. They fell behind on the mortgage payments, despite such emergency measures as selling the $5,000 cherry armoire for $380. Behind on the mortgage— that didn't seem like a huge problem; Washington politicians were practically offering prizes for falling behind on a mortgage. But Tom and Margo had bought into the complex without fully comprehending that the homeowners' association held a lien for dues. Tom skipped the association-dues payment, thinking he'd make it up later, and the homeowners' association immediately filed for foreclosure. Later he learned the "association," owned by a Florida investor, had foreclosed on the townhome they purchased, then resold it at a profit, four times in the past two years. Tom was furious at himself for missing such a detail, something he'd never done before—for making the sort of mistake made by people who do their grocery shopping at 7-Eleven.

"Sorry," Margo said into the landline after redialing the cell. "Twenty-six minutes on hold and now I have to go through the voice prompts all over. I was calling the cable company to disconnect. Press one to go on hold; press two to be disconnected; press three to hear these options again. If you're buying something they put you right through. If you're trying to cancel they never pick up and I'm sure the machine is programmed to 'accidentally' disconnect. These deals that say 'cancel at any time,' you can't cancel because you can't get through."

The apartment building was a set of doors into lives about which Margo knew little. She always hurried through the halls to reach her place and get in before running into other tenants, and noted other tenants seemed to do the same. They did not want to have to get to know the sort of people who would live in the sort of building where they lived. Margo imagined many tenants told themselves, "I don't belong in a building like this." If you got to know the other tenants, then it was like you belonged.

The window looked out onto a warehouse parking lot, where bright anticrime lights shined the whole night long. Tom had gotten frustrated trying to hang blinds correctly, and they couldn't pay a handyman. So for the moment, towels held by pushpin tacks were the solution when it was time to make the apartment dark enough for sleeping. The old house had window treatments selected by a decorating consultant. Margo's college dorm room had proper blinds. Her girlhood bedroom had blinds, embroidered draperies, and blackout curtains for sleeping late on weekends. This apartment had towels held in place by tacks.

"So the counselor tells me Caroline has been called to the office twice this month for wardrobe. I did not know she was leaving here in one outfit then taking clothes off in the washroom when she got to school. We had a screaming fight about the tank tops and her belly button always showing." Margo paused to listen. "No she's not acting out an issue in our marriage!" She listened again. "I don't understand why they don't freeze either. In the mall these teen girls have nothing on; the boys are in shorts when it's snowing. Why aren't they freezing? Some kind of genetic mutation has made the next generation impervious to cold."

On the feet of the contemporary teen girls were boots, even in warm weather. Their feet and ankles were the only body parts well covered. At high school and the malls, teen girls showed lots of skin. At parties the girls would come as close to naked as possible—hot pants with tank tops or very short black dresses that barely covered their behinds. Margo wondered how teen boys could stand it—how did boys pumped with hormones function in this environment?

Perhaps it was an unconscious group evolutionary fitness strategy on the part of girls. Since around the time the slut look came into fashion—and began being tolerated by the moms who bought the clothes—girls' grades and college admission rates had soared while boys' grades and college admission rates went down. Williams College, a generation ago all-male, now was 53 percent female; the University of Georgia was 62 percent female; two out of three bachelor's degrees were being awarded to women. Education is the key to future economic power, and girls and young women were significantly outperforming boys and young men in this contest. Keeping the teen boys staring at their legs in class, unable to focus, conferred a selection advantage.

As she talked on the landline, Margo methodically punched buttons on the cell phone to go through the voice prompt, which kept asking different versions of the same questions and for repetition of information already entered. The repetition was intended to get callers irritated so they would hang up. Modern corporate voice-prompt 800 numbers ask your name, address and account number half a dozen times before finally putting on the line an agent whose first question is your name, address and account number. No matter how often you say "agent" or "representative," the voice prompts drone on, with the same questions over and over. After fifteen minutes or so the voice prompt finally will ask if you want to speak to someone, as if this outcome were an unprecedented surprise. The computer voice prompts are always so chipper—"Hi, I'm Julie, I'm here to help you." Of course they are not here to help you.

Margo's landline phone call continued: "And Megan, I never should have given in on ears pierced at twelve, now she wants her tongue pierced. She's not doing well in school either, and Megan was reading

The Grapes of Wrath in fifth grade." She paused to listen. "What—that's what she wants the pierced tongue for? Yes, I bet it would increase her popularity! I'm going to have to confront Megan. Just what I need, another confrontation. I considered taking the girls to counseling. But . . . we are kind of between health plans right now. Changing schools twice in three years cannot have helped."

They had picked the new apartment because it was in the best school district they could afford. A decent high school, nothing special—at least no metal detectors at the main entrance. Tom was driving an hour each way to his job in order to put them there. Margo had gone back to work. She had not worked as a waitress since the summer of her sophomore year. If you'd told her then she would be waitressing again two decades later, she'd have fainted.

Margo tried to find something in finance. Her qualifications were solid, but as it was the big banks and investment houses were laying off staff even as they awarded their executives multimillion-dollar bonuses that were subsidized by the federal deficit. The payments were justified as "retention" bonuses to prevent the executives from jumping to other jobs. Since there were no other jobs in finance at the moment, this was a transparent ruse. Members of Congress nodded in assent, in return for campaign donations.

Serving men vodka at eleven-thirty in the morning and flirting like mad in the hope they would leave a five-dollar bill—that had not been Margo's life plan for this point. Maybe, she mused, I should have Caroline pick my outfits, to increase tips. Margo worked the lunch rush, not dinner, so as to finish in time to meet the girls at school. She parked a block away and they walked to her so their friends would not know what car Margo was driving.

"All these years of grooming them to be doctors or university deans," Margo said into the landline. "Now one behaves like her career aspiration is to be a part-time barista while the other wants to work street corners. It's the constant message of appearances, the superficiality and cheap sex they are exposed to in the culture. And who's behind the constant messages of superficiality and cheap sex? Not radical artists. Corporate America: Comcast, Disney, Nike, Fox."

The cell phone clicked and clunked. "Wait, I have to call you back, I finally just got through."

Margo rung off the landline, picked up the cell and began to speak. "Hi, I need to cancel my cable.

My account number is—fuck!" She slammed down the cell phone. The connection had broken the instant she finally was put through to an agent. "Fuck, fuck, fuck, fuck, fuck!"

Kevin was in the living room, watching television. When he heard her repeating "fuck" over and over he came to the door arch and asked, "You all right, Mrs. H?"

"Why—yes! Yes of course." In addition to being angry, Margo was now embarrassed.

"So it's true about women's fantasies," Kevin said.

"Sorry?"

"I was reading the *National Enquirer* last night at the Burger More," Kevin replied. "I went in for a Double Mega and a Phake Shake. This story said a famous psychologist had proven modern women constantly fantasize about—"

"Oh!" Margo laughed. "Actually women fantasize about square footage, winning the White House . . . those sorts of things. Sex, too. But mostly about conquering the world."

A few hours after meeting Kevin at the convention center, Tom had been fired. The Bayliner woman not only complained vociferously, she stormed into the executive office area to complain, despite the secretaries insisting no one could enter without an appointment and of course, appointments never were granted. She got all the way to the office of the Associate Deputy Administrator for Administration—the only high-ranking official actually present that day—before security escorted her back to the convention floor. The Associate Deputy Administrator for Administration was furious about being confronted in his office, where he'd been using his laptop to watch a Bruce Willis movie while filing paperwork for early retirement at age forty-six; his plan was to activate his pension, then return to the same job and double-dip. Half the top figures in the city and county government were double-dipping, the other half awaiting the first possible legal day to do so. Shouting about incompetent Facilitators, the Associate Deputy Administrator for Administration ordered that heads roll.

Eleven government employees with lifetime job security, funded by borrowing, had to sign Tom's dismissal notice. He supposed the entire executive-suite staff at the convention center, perhaps fifty people, did nothing for an entire day except fire him.

A week later Tom took a job selling fiber-optic Internet and television services from a mall booth. Not even a store—a glorified pushcart in a mall's foot-traffic flow. The pushcart was decorated with screens that were supposed to simulate high-def images; there were clipboards with contracts for the marks to sign. Tom was fired from the pushcart job after the local sales manager, whose pay was a percentage of each salesperson's commission, found out Tom helped a young Hispanic couple who didn't seem to have much money read the details of the offer. He suspected they needed other things a lot more than the "Platinum Package" with twenty-five premium-price channels. Once they understood the terms, the young couple walked. Once the local manager knew that, Tom was cashiered.

The last thing a corporation wants is for anyone to read the disclaimers. Many disclaimers are in all-caps six-point type to discourage reading. In disclaimers, warranties and similar quasilegal documents, all-caps does not mean "this is the important part." All-caps means this is the part they want to make sure you can't read. The first line of most disclaimers might as well say, PLEASE DO NOT READ BEFORE SIGNING.

Before Tom was fired from the pushcart job, Kevin had wandered by. He and Tom got to talking and later went out for a beer. Margo understood that Kevin had been living the dismissal-to-dismissal lifestyle, and Tom felt sympathy; but in retrospect, she wished Tom hadn't given Kevin his cell number. When Kevin was tossed from an SRO, tumbling even further down the breakwater of life, he showed up at Tom and Margo's apartment, asking for a few nights on the couch. A few nights became a few weeks. Margo was far from happy regarding this, especially with teen daughters in the same small space.

"My first wife, Donna, didn't fantasize about anything; mainly she tried to think of ways we could keep the house," Kevin said. Margo winced. Kevin had already told her this many times.

"It must have been hard for you when she got sick," Margo said. She looked intently at the papers on the table, trying to send the message that she was busy.

"We should have given up and sold the house sooner," Kevin said. "That way she could have gotten the operation while there was still time."

"You didn't know." *Many, many times.* Kevin talked about himself almost exclusively, and Kevin's life entailed events that soap-opera scriptwriters would have rejected as clichéd.

"Before they would do the operation, the hospital

insisted we sign the house over to them. I waited too long. I should have just signed it over. When I finally tried, they knew the foreclosure had already started. They told me to find a cosigner! Who was I supposed to get, the pope?"

"You mustn't reproach yourself. You did everything you could."

"She talks to me sometimes," Kevin said. "I mean, I'm not crazy. But I believe Donna can see me and is trying to guide my life. I hear her whisper to me about what the baby would have been like. Which lotto numbers to play. That kind of thing."

"I am sure she was a remarkable person."

"My second wife, Gigi, she did think about fucking all the time. Just not with me."

"She was a foolish woman, then."

"Hey, thanks Mrs. H. You're stand-up. You know that?"

"Donna wants you to get back on your feet," Margo said. "Donna wants you to get a job and find your own place."

"Between the debt to Donna's hospice and the alimony to Gigi, I'm stuck behind the eight ball. Even when I'm working, most of the paycheck is garnished.

That's how me and Tom got to be friends. We'd both lost houses and were both headed down the toilet financially. Gave us something in common."

These were not agreeable words for Margo to hear. She saw Kevin as someone her generous husband had encountered by chance and generously offered to assist on a temporary basis. Tom told her, "I meet a man in need, how can I not act?" A narrative like that worked for Margo as an explanation of Tom extending his hand. That narrative involved a good deed, a mitzvah. But there was no sign of Kevin getting on his feet. And the notion of Tom and Kevin becoming friends with commonality alarmed Margo deeply.

"Tom will bounce back soon," she said.

"Oh, he will! He's got the degree, that way of talking, of pretending he's interested in what you are saying. I guess in college you get a lot of experience acting nice to people you can't stand. That's a valuable life skill."

"I'm sure you would have done well in college, Kevin. You have practical intelligence."

"Tom is my inspiration. I wish I had his way to stay calm and talk calm." Kevin wasn't sure what to call poise, and didn't have much experience with it. "When they laid us off at the drop-ship facility, I wanted to ram a broom up that corporate guy's ass. I know I shouldn't of screamed that I would cut the brake lines on his car. But that was no cause to arrest me, nobody thought I really meant it. Man, I was steamed. I'd been there two years and not one day of severance. I still don't understand how they got away with giving us nothing."

"They put the firm's assets under a new name in a spinoff corporation headquartered in the Caymans, then had the old firm declared bankrupt, voiding debts to bondholders and obligations to workers. One week prior, they issued $80 million in bonuses to top management," Margo said.

She remembered the options traders she once worked with, who considered that sort of thing perfectly normal—pilfer from investors and labor, place the proceeds into the pockets of insiders. Bernard Madoff wasn't some weird exception—rather, a man who took common Wall Street practices a tad too far. Enron's bogus accounting caused $63 billion of other people's money to vanish, while Enron executives rolled in wealth and political influence. Jeffrey Skilling, the former Enron president convicted of securities fraud, was arguing on appeal that systematic lying for personal gain does not constitute fraud because it is normal procedure in the corporate world. The sophisticated investor should expect to be lied to! After elite money firms AIG, Bear Stearns, Lehman Brothers and Merrill Lynch were exposed in 2008 as wood-paneled con jobs, no one from these organizations went to jail. The banker or corporate executive who lies to the public while lining his pockets knows he may someday be caught and embarrassed, but also knows there never will be any criminal consequences, and he'll keep the funds he stole. The scandal is not what corporations do in violation of law. The scandal is what they do legally.

"They sure screwed the average guy," Kevin said of his old employer. Margo couldn't think of any useful reply. Wall Street cheers when corporations lay off workers and shift to offshore tax havens, as this drives up profit. People didn't realize Ronald Reagan had been wise when he said, "Never confuse Wall Street with the economy."

"When I got that job in the air-bag factory, I figured I was set," Kevin continued. *Many, many times.* "The way people drive, air bags will always be needed, right? But they closed the plant. Now the air bags are made in Bhutan."

"You're not supposed to question market forces," Margo said.

"Some dad puts his daughter into a car and tells her, 'Don't worry, kid, if there's ever a crash, the air bag from Bhutan will save you. It's got cutting-edge Bhutanese technology.'"

As they talked, Kevin nosed around the kitchen, trying to do so unobtrusively, looking for something to drink. Margo had forbidden him to bring alcohol into the apartment—the girls, after all. He went out to drink many nights: she'd told him if he came in obviously drunk again, he would be back on the street, no discussion. A drunken stranger in an apartment home to two teen girls—Margo shuddered. Kevin shied away from Caroline and Megan, knowing the mother grizzly was near. What distressed Margo was placing the girls in the same close environment as a failed person, one who represented the life choices she wanted her girls to have nothing to do with.

"Every day the business section of the newspaper disturbs me," Margo said. Avoiding friends from her former social circle, because she wanted to avoid discussion of money problems, Margo found herself having conversations with Kevin, and that was another bad sign. "Maytag closed its factories in Illinois. Russell Stover closed one of its chocolate factories—we've even outsourced the candy. Now there are no longer any television sets or typewriters made in the United States."

"People still use typewriters?"

"Jobs are disappearing left and right, yet every year there are more waterfront developments with trendy restaurants," Margo said. She knew the statistics about rising top-tier income and net worth—the same economic forces that made iPhones and DVRs affordable were concentrating wealth at the top. Once those forces smiled on Margo's family; now they were turned against her. It was nothing personal.

Back when Margo dined in the trendy restaurants, she didn't stop to think that average people were losing jobs to make her lifestyle happen. Now it seemed to her like the economy had become a food chain with nothing at the bottom. So should imports be banned, forcing everyone to buy products that cost more? If factory productivity improvements were barred by law, there would be more jobs for steelworkers and autoworkers, but the country's standard of living would decline. That would hit average people a lot harder than it would hit the top 1 percent.

Kevin found Tom's vodka but left it alone after a hard glance from Margo. He took some Ritz crackers and began putting grape jelly on them.

"The jobs going to China," he said, "you don't think the Chinese planned it that way, do you? They know they can't beat our military. They know their movies will never be as popular as ours. They know they will never even get near our pizza. They know that if you want to eat a pizza, watch a movie and hit something with a bomb, the United States will always be the only game in town. USA! USA! So they put on this big smile and say, sure, we'll do your manufacturing for you at half the price. Our CEOs agree, that way they can pump up their stock options, then quit just before the prosecutors arrive. Our politicians agree, that way the lobbyists keep giving them campaign contributions. One day the Chinese government will call up our government and say, 'So sorry, but we now have you by the'—how do you say 'balls' in Chinese?"

"I have a feeling we are going to find out."

When Margo lived in a beautiful house and drank expensive Cabernets, she and her friends would sit discussing what a disgrace it was that government and churches did not do more for those whose luck was hard. Especially the churches, which claimed to exist for the purpose of extending a hand. All denominations of all faiths spend far more on themselves than on the needy. As her own fortunes declined, Margo was doing something she never would have considered when she lived well: allowing a hard-luck victim to share her home. She realized that before, she didn't notice people like Kevin. Her eyes passed over without her seeing them. Now it was as if they glowed.

"Anyway, don't worry about Tom," Kevin said. "That pharmaceutical start-up he worked at, how was he supposed to know they had been testing the medicine on African orphans?"

"Last night Tom called himself 'a loser in life's contest.'"

"No way. I've known a lot bigger losers than Tom," Kevin replied cheerfully.

Margo wanted to cry—both to hear these words and because she was having this conversation with Kevin. He continued, "Besides, Tom is hardworking, good-looking, law-abiding and well educated. There should be at least another ten years where there are still jobs for people like that."

This whole line of discussion had to stop, but Margo was too well mannered to just tell Kevin to shut up. "When the jobs are gone," she said, "what happens next, the robots take over?"

"I'm guessing clones," Kevin said. "Robots sound expensive. Clones could have sex and reproduce for free. Regular humanity would become expendable. That's pretty much where trends are headed already anyway."

Margo thought about that and said, "My worry is Western civilization ends when a runaway cloning experiment inadvertently creates thousands of Kardashian sisters."

Kevin brightened, saying, "That sounds great!"

To Margo's relief, the key turned. Tom entered, wearing the uniform of a package-delivery service. He looked tired and seemed winded. "Sorry, need to catch my breath," he said. "Those stairs."

"I called the super about the elevator," Margo said. Then, thinking about him winded, said, "You know, Tom, you haven't had a physical in years." She bit her tongue the moment she said this.

"We don't have health insurance—why waste money for a doctor to tell me I was young once and am not anymore? Believe me, I know the sweetness of youth is gone."

Tom seemed to age just by saying this. To Margo, he had always appeared boyish, even when he put on a monochrome business suit and left for meetings. In the last three years he had changed to graying, by appearances skipping middle age entirely.

"If you wait until you're about to die, then you can go to the emergency room free," Kevin said in a chipper way, as if this were "news you can use."

"The president is pushing a reform bill," Margo said.

"Years will pass before the new bill takes effect," Kevin replied. "Till then, same old same old. Lots of people depend on waiting till they get sick, so they can get treated free in the emergency room. That's how it works."

"Listen to him, he knows," Tom said, slightly darkly.

"If you're just trying to stay healthy, doctors and hospitals are allowed to turn you away," Kevin said. "If you're bleeding or having a heart attack, law says the hospital must treat you. So guys on construction crews, nannies whose last names the householders don't even know—instead of getting low-cost treatment while a condition is preventable, they wait till it's a crisis, then head to the emergency room."

"He knows," Tom repeated.

"Check it out, once you've got an emergency, cost is no object." Kevin began to sound like the host of a middle-of-the-night talk-radio show airing only in his head.

He proceeded: "If you're lucky, you get a helicopter ride. I did once. Had this temperature of a hundred and three, knew if I went to any doctor's office I'd be turned away. So I called 911 and said I'd just come back from a National Geographic expedition in Africa and thought I was exposed to Ebola. They sent a *helicopter*, a red one like in a disaster movie. It was really cool. If I ever owned a helicopter I would definitely want red. I'd want everyone to see me, I'd be like—yo, here I am in my helicopter, how's it feel to be on the ground? These cops came first and marked a landing area with flares to guide the chopper in. I felt important. That ride musta cost five grand. Not sure who paid—it wasn't me. The American medical system will spend twenty thousand dollars fixing what could have been prevented for twenty bucks. But if you only need generic tetracycline for your upper respiratory, they won't give you bus fare."

"He knows what he's talking about," Tom said.

Suddenly Tom became Kevin's sidekick on the radio show: "Forcing people to wait until routine conditions become emergencies creates patients who need expensive procedures. The hospital companies and the specialists benefit." Tom seemed to have given the issue some thought. As he spoke, Margo realized Tom had been talking about the health-care legislation debate quite a bit, while following the details closely.

"Janitors can't get a bottle of Advil, cleaning ladies can't get a mammogram," Kevin said. "But a heart-lung transplant? Decade on life support? No problem!" It was as though they could hear rock music swelling up—nearly time to go to commercial. Kevin continued with brio. "If everybody had access to some regular doc for regular care, there would be less suffering, but spending would go down. Not as many emergencies sent to specialists. That would be bad news for the big medical companies. Why do you think they're fighting reform?"

A good talk-radio spiel, Kevin knew from listening to the kinds of hosts who come on after midnight, always builds up to a conspiracy driven by money.

"I refuse to be so cynical as to believe doctors don't want to keep people well," Margo said.

We've got Margo on line one. Hello, Margo, you're on

Kevin's Korner. "Sure, some people say the docs are honest. But open your eyes. Think about it from the point of view of Big Pharma and the surgeons. Big Pharma has CEOs who expect bonuses for sitting in a chair. The surgeons expect a new Mercedes every year. From their perspective, ideally nobody would have health insurance. Then everybody would be dying of something, and business would be great!"

Tom slapped his hand on the table and said, "Change the subject!" There was silence in the apartment.

Chapter 8

July 2009

Unemployment: 9.3 percent.
Home foreclosures hit all-time high.
500,000 Afghans and Iraqis dead
in U.S. retaliation for 3,000 American deaths.

Sixteen up! Repeating order sixteen is up!"

Order 16, the starters for a four-top—deep-fried mozzarella, blue-cheese sliders, batter-coated buffalo wings and potato skins baked with bacon and cheddar—had been at the window for a good ninety seconds, which was too long. Up orders were supposed to depart for the table within sixty seconds. That way they'd be sizzling when placed before the customer, who in any case was in a hurry to eat. People complained if food did not begin arriving a few minutes after they gave their selections.

Though the chain's TV ads depicted smiling multicultural friends laughing through a leisurely repast without a care in the world, waitresses were supposed to do everything in their power to speed the turnover of tables. Take orders quickly, bring food and drink quickly, clear plates and present checks quickly. During dinner, the average table was thirty-one minutes from seating to departure; during lunch, twenty-three minutes. And waitstaff was to push, push, push those 1,500-calorie desserts, since fifty cents' worth of sugar, butter and chocolate could be sold for $7.95 as long as the concoction was huge, which connotes value. True value in an era of national obesity would be a tasty small dessert that salved the sweet tooth but contained reasonable calories. That's not how the contemporary American restaurant customer thinks. Value is a gigantic dish, the sort that causes busboys to ask, "Are you still working on that?"

The buffalo wings were listed on the menu not just as buffalo wings but as Xtreme Buffalo Wing Explosion. The sliders were listed as Bacon Blue Blast Bonanza Sliders. Staff weren't supposed to call the dishes by their commons names, rather, always to use the promotional names—not to say "I need an order of sliders," rather "I need an order of Bacon Blue Blast Bonanza Sliders." Using the long names slowed down what was intended to be a rapid process. The directive to say the long names came from a marketing executive at corporate headquarters who'd written a memo declaring everything in the chain's facilities, even napkins and cocktail sticks, should be branded. Modern executives often were more concerned with pushing the brand than pushing the product, which didn't necessarily say much for the product.

Video cameras at the restaurant watched not only the parking lot and dining areas but the kitchen, bar and staff break room. A miniature camera at the hostess station used video facial analytics to rate hostesses on whether they smiled enough. Audio monitors in the kitchen and bus areas employed software to listen for key words such as "union" and "organize," alerting the regional manager whenever key words were heard. The key-word software knew Spanish and was learning Urdu.

Software developed by twenty-five-year-old Caltech grads at a Silicon Valley start-up analyzed images from the video feeds. If the silhouette of a person stopped moving in the staff break room for more than five minutes—the maximum break the chain's rules allowed—the manager on-site received a text message

generated by a computer. He had sixty seconds to respond to the text message, or would receive a demerit
for the day. The silhouette had another sixty seconds
beyond that to resume moving, or that person would
be placed on probation.

The Caltech grads who designed this monitor-
ing software themselves mainly played videogames at
work. Their system was already viewed by some corporate cost-cutting consultants as obsolescent. Under development were tiny radio-frequency pins to be worn
by staff, each with a unique ID the computer could
track. This would allow employees to be monitored on
the speed and efficiency of all movements. A waitress
who stood by the bartender station rather than circu-
lating among the tables, for example, would be noti-
fied during her shift that headquarters knew she was
not working hard enough. Version 2.0 of the radio-
frequency device would monitor employees' speech,
creating a log of every offense from failing to ask "Do
you want to mega-size?" to criticizing the corporation
while on its property.

The eatery chain's name was Feels Like Home.

"Sixteen up! Third request!"

Margo hustled for the tray. That table ordered a

round of martinis at 11:15 A.M. The bartender didn't quite have the well set up so early, slowing down the drink preparation and thus slowing Margo down. She noted the manager scowling and pointing at his watch as she carted the appetizers to the table.

All four men had asked for different types of vodka in their martinis. Though vodka is flavorless, those at the table had been discoursing, as they ordered, on whether Grey Goose or Skyy or Absolut "tastes best." This meant the bartender had to mark each drink so Margo could tell them apart, not that there was a chance in the world anyone at the table would be able to determine, by sipping, whether he'd been served the requested brand. As the men held forth about the vodkas, trying to demonstrate deep knowledge, Margo batted her eyes and tilted her head—flirting cues— and wondered if she could get them to leave a twenty as the tip.

One might think restaurants and big-box stores would be pleased with the cool economy causing the white-collar cohort to seek jobs for which they normally don't compete. Instead there was some resentment by those who had never been white-collar. Margo's manager gave her a hard time over minor slips that he ignored in others. He launched zingers, such as asking where she parked her BMW. Though a little dictator within the province of the restaurant, the manager scrupulously avoided any act or comment that might be construed as sexual, as groping and sexist remarks are changing from a management prerogative to a career-killer within business culture. A generation ago, someone in Margo's position would have been taken to a back room, told to shut up, then felt up, and been afraid to complain. Today someone in her position received class-warfare insults. Progress.

"How's the drinks, guys?" Margo asked, tilting her head and shaking her hair. "Strong enough for big guys like you?" Men stepping out, she'd found, like to be addressed as guys. Margo leaned forward, to draw attention to her décolletage. The guys smiled.

Looking up, Margo beheld what waitresses dread in the way that fishermen dread a high wave approaching from the side of the boat. A dozen people were arriving as a group. No one had called ahead, so nothing was set up. Big parties get huffy quickly about service, expect the waitress to jump straight up into the air, and generate clamor as if no additional patrons were present, disturbing other diners. They do this though the diners at the big table would be outraged if they were trying to have a quiet evening and someone else arrived and started making loud noise.

Often when a large group sits together in a restaurant, one or many toss in less than the average cost shown on the bill, then find it convenient to assume someone else is treating for the gratuity. Irresponsible? They live in a society where citizens angrily demand that government spending go down while angrily demanding a rise in whatever benefits they personally receive.

As the group was directed toward tables being rearranged into a single seating in Margo's section, she went to the manager to ask him to greet them and impose the single-check 18-percent-added policy. Fancy restaurants do this as a matter of course. Dinner-house chains in the middle of the market impose the mandatory gratuity at the manager's discretion. The manager wouldn't, telling Margo it was her problem to deal with the group. She felt sure he would have done this to help other waitresses. There was a nasty twinkle in his eye, as if he could see ahead to an hour during which Margo would work frantically, only to be stiffed.

She headed to the large group and swallowed hard. "My name is Margo, I'll be your server today—"

There was a greeting script that she hated, but knowing the manager was eavesdropping, Margo went through it. All the women were talking at once, so none heard her. After she finished reciting the specials, the first question was "What are your specials?"

Margo took their drink orders, and a short time later had the busboy help her carry the drinks back. She raised her pad to ask what they wanted for lunch.

"The fettuccine—how is it prepared?"

"I would like an appetizer-sized portion of the dinner ravioli and a dinner-sized portion of the stuffed mushrooms appetizer."

"Are peanuts used in the cooking area?"

"Can you give me a half-sized steak at half price?"

"I want the Greek salad with no olives and no feta cheese."

"Do you accept coupons from T.G.I. Friday's? We have coupons from there."

"What ingredients are in the lasagna?"

"I don't see tapas on the menu. Can you make a tapas platter for us?"

"Does the coq au vin come with chicken?"

"Oprah says not to eat corn-based sweetener. Which of your dishes contain no corn-based sweeteners?"

"Why haven't you brought the bread yet?"

"My seat faces the kitchen door."

"You're not feeding us anything genetically altered, are you?"

"I felt a draft."

"Why do you serve fermented products?"

"Do you have gluten-free bread?"

"There's a spot on my knife."

"It's too hot."

"It's too cold."

"What are your specials?"

"The service here is terrible."

Minutes had passed and none of the ladies had placed her order. Mentally, Margo heard a clock ticking—other tables were sure to need attention by now. The front door opened and in came a couple who were obviously arguing. They were leading a sobbing three-year-old and carrying a crying infant in a rocker. The arrivals were shown to a table in Margo's section. They sat, waving to Margo as if in dire need. Simultaneously one of the four guys, already on their second round before the clock struck noon, made a broad gesture with his hand and knocked his martini into the drink of the guy next to him, vodka flowing in all directions. From the kitchen Margo heard, "Lunch for sixteen is up! Up!"

Margo gestured to the busboy about the guys with the spilled drinks; informed the ladies she'd be right back ("Now she's leaving. I *told* you we shouldn't have come here"); grabbed crayons and paper to drop on the table of the arguing couple; got the lunch order for 16, timing her arrival just as the busboy finished cleaning the table; promised the guys a third round on the house, wincing to herself at the thought of serving a third martini at noon; hoisted bread and butter for the ladies, plus a new silverware set wrapped in a napkin for the woman who complained about the knife. Twice she had to calculate which hand to hold an item in—whether it would be faster to put down the item in her right hand to pick up something else then pick the item up again or to use her left and right hands at the same time.

At the restaurant, a lot of Margo's brain volume was assigned to making snap judgments about what order to pick up and put down, to maximize efficiency in the relocation of beers and Caesar salads. If you already had three things in one hand and two in the other, putting all five down to move a sixth thing, then picking the first five up again, was way too time-consuming for the lunch-rush environment. She had learned to use one hand only while keeping everything else in whatever hand already held most. Once, juggling many things, she tried to save an instant by putting a bill folder, the black wallets in which checks are delivered, in her mouth. The manager spied that and chewed her out. Okay, she shouldn't have. But Margo was offended that her mouth, the most sensuous part of a woman, the place so many boys and men had wanted to get, now was objectionable.

Margo felt a dull bolt in her lower back, low-voltage pain announcing that high-voltage pain would arrive by the shift's end. She had begun to take an Advil when reporting to the restaurant, not waiting to see if she'd need one later, just assuming she would—the way football players take painkillers before a game when they are feeling fine, because they know it's only a matter of time until they don't feel fine. Six things to carry precariously balanced in her hands, she heard one of the ladies calling, "Miss! Miss! What's taking so long!"

For a moment, Margo worried she would lose her composure. She reminded herself she should only be doing this a short time, that the establishment and many like it were staffed by people who'd spent their lives on their feet trying to meet impatient demands. Margo was pretty good at controlling her own disappointments with thoughts like that. Would she still be good at controlling her disappointments if the family's situation remained the same well into the future?

An hour passed in which Margo worked as hard as she had in her life, as hard as when she stayed up studying for finals; as hard as the night, as a summer counselor in Wisconsin, when the camp-out tent collapsed in a downpour and she led a group of frightened little girls on a mile-long, middle-of-the-night hike back to the lodge through forest in sideways rain.

At the end of the hour the ladies asked for individual checks. Margo said no, and they reacted as if she had lunged at them with a carving knife.

Though they had ordered starters and a number of frou-frou cocktails, the women were outraged that the bill came to $300, before tip. That was $25 per head for drinks, lunch and dessert—what did they expect? Several declared they hadn't possibly spent more than $10. Margo went over the bill line by line, showing it added up to $300. Several among the group claimed to have no cash, just cards or a checkbook, and again demanded separate bills. After the ladies nearly pitched a fit, Margo gave in and split the checks into twelve. This meant quite a bit of added effort—figuring the twelve bills, then doing as many card slips or making change. Nine of the twelve left her nothing, several drawing multiple lines through the "tip" space on the card invoice. Two left a dollar apiece, perhaps viewing themselves as great benefactors of humanity. One left pocket change. The result was a $2.68 tip on a $300 tab.

Attending to her other tables, Margo saw one of the ladies have a heated discussion with the manager, then strut out. As the lunch rush wound down, the manager called Margo to his "office"—a room where crates of tomato sauce and ketchup were stacked. One crate was labeled EXTRA-HEAVY MAYONNAISE.

"The large party you had today complained about your service," he told her.

"I busted my ass for them. You saw me."

"They also complained about your attitude. Said they noticed you making a face in their direction." The manager had a rack on which hung the orange-and-brown shirts of the chain. He had several, all identical.

"'Making a face'? What, is there facecrime now?" The manager had no idea what she meant, and if she'd told him she was referencing the novel *1984*, would have been offended that she was hinting he'd not gone to college.

"The customer is king. We cannot have unsatisfied customers," he said plainly.

"I busted my ass for them, and they left a three-dollar tip on a three-hundred-dollar tab. People like that should be arrested."

"See, that's attitude. Tips are not guaranteed. Tips are rewards for exceptional service."

"I gave them exceptional service! And you pay $2.13 an hour on the assumption that all customers tip."

"Plus she said you were a slut."

"*What?*"

"They saw you flirting with a table full of men when you should have been waiting on them. Her exact words were that she and her friends would never come back to a restaurant where the waitresses are sluts."

Margo tried to stay calm. "Anyone that mean has issues. Those bitches don't need lunch, they need therapists."

"See, now you are using profanity to describe our valued customers. I'm sorry, Margo. Have to let you go."

There was no point arguing. Margo left in time to pick up the girls from school, saying nothing about what happened.

Chapter 9

August 2009

Japanese recession ends; lasted 18 years.
United States debt for a single decade exceeds all
borrowing in the country's previous
211 years of existence.

Margo sat at the kitchen table of the apartment with the Help Wanted section of the newspaper open next to her. Once the Help Wanted section was thick, going on for page after page; now, it seemed barely the size of the tables of sports scores. Of course, some job adverts had migrated to the Web. On her laptop, Margo was scanning Craigslist and Monster under employment openings. When Margo first typed Monster in the Google search box, she found the website of a company that makes high-end audio equipment, then that of a firm that makes energy drinks, thereby learning there are three corporations named

Monster, the employment agency and two others. Three big corporations that present themselves to the world as monsters. This means something. Perhaps best not to know what.

Kevin had been tossed out, after spending what he had on shots and beers, then coming in stumbling drunk in front of the girls. Margo felt bad about tossing him, in the way one feels bad when hearing of natural disasters in countries one could not locate on a map. She did not feel bad enough to relent.

Margo looked nervously at her cell phone. One of her daughters was at a party, the other "out with friends," her only explanation. Margo provided both with cell phones, despite increasing problems covering the bill. They protested that the phones were merely phones, not smart phones—unable to receive the Internet, satellite guidance or live video. Web access would be another thirty dollars per month per phone, plus numerous mysterious taxes—sorry, not taxes, "fees." That would be nearly a thousand dollars per year just so the girls could Facebook from a Starbucks. Once Margo would have agreed to such a small luxury without hesitation. Now it was a budget buster.

Margo texted each of the girls once every hour and fretted if they didn't text back within minutes. She

did not care what incomprehensible codes they used—
"smh s/b 7 k?"—as long as they texted back.

Summer meant no school, which meant more op-
portunities for the girls to get into trouble. Not just
the getting-into-trouble kind of trouble mothers always worry about. The sorts of bad choices that teens
have been making in private since time immemorial
now go public with a click: the teen who posts a Facebook photo of herself dancing topless by a pool will
still be dealing with that minor misjudgment in twenty
years. Technology offered all manner of new, innovative trouble.

The day was hot and the window air conditioner,
thrumming loudly, was losing its battle against the
heat. Margo stood by the strident machine to feel
dried air caress her neck. The dried air was welcome
in two ways, as cooling and as a sensation delivered
from skin.

Tom rarely touched her now, and she didn't think
the cause was her—Margo still had her looks and still
had reasonably close to a young woman's figure. The
cause was Tom. He was working himself to exhaustion
in humdrum jobs, staring off into space when they
were together. Margo thought he could benefit from
counseling but financially that was out of the question.

She turned the air-conditioner control to maximum. The output felt no colder.

Tom opened the door, breathing hard. He'd sweated through his delivery-service outfit. Tom was a driver now, not just a jumper, and hoping to have his own jumper in November. With Christmas creep—radio stations going all-Christmas-music around Veterans Day, Black Friday sales starting before Thanksgiving, Christmas lights up before the last leaves of autumn were raked—most drivers had help by mid-November. But that was months to come. A driver working a delivery truck solo was his own jumper, so all shift long, Tom bolted from the truck to the drop-off and bolted back.

Tom saw that Margo noticed all the sweat; it was warm out, but he hadn't exactly been playing basketball. He was aware Margo noticed his labored breathing.

She hugged him, and wondered what couples who have been together a long time often wonder—should I try to Talk, or just talk? One of the joys of a long-term relationship is that your partner spares you freighted conversation, and Margo was aware of her obligations to Tom in this regard.

"Baby, it scares me when you get like this," Margo

said. Calling him "baby" took a little edge off. When the young and fancy-free Margo called a man "baby," this meant she was in the mood to be on her back or her knees. Calling Tom "baby" had meant that for twenty years, just not lately.

"You being winded, this has been happening. You know better than me. Surely you should—"

"I don't need to pay a doctor to look at my date of birth and tell me my age."

"Shortness of breath is a specific symptom, Tom."

He sat down and pushed the shoes off his feet. Margo could smell perspiration in Tom's socks. She saw dried blood on one of his heels, where he must have developed a blister.

"I should be in better shape, I'm running all day long," Tom said.

When he needed pants now he bought them over the Internet or went to a store alone, so Margo wouldn't know his waist size. There were faint crinkles on his neck, skin no longer taut—the subtle declines of middle age, in their way worse than the obvious ones. Anyone in middle age knows the sweetness of youth has passed. But until the evidence appears in the mirror, this topic can be avoided. As Tom looked out of his own eyes, he saw the world exactly as he'd seen the world when he could stay up till three A.M., when he could run five miles, when his stomach was lumber-flat, when the sight of Margo in a towel made him erect in seconds.

The mind behind Tom's eyes thought in the same way it had in youth, and carried the same hopes. For his life until this point, Tom had been capable, lean, attractive to women, on his way up in the world. Since adolescence, this was the only condition he'd known. When Tom looked out through his eyes, he was watching the same movie he had watched all his life, of a fascinating world awaiting discovery. Looking outward, from his perspective nothing had changed. But now when Tom looked into the mirror, he saw the indicators of decline. The movie of the great world will always be playing. How much longer would he be in the audience?

"I didn't realize they made you run with the packages."

"Run from the truck to the door. Any package less than twenty pounds, you're supposed to run. Coming back from the door without a package, always run. Every day you're rated on seconds per delivery. The only way to finish the route on time is to run. That's why we wear shorts even on cool days, prevent overheating

from running. No friendly chatting with customers—
stop to chat and your seconds-per-delivery drops." Tom
had noted the delivery drivers running back and forth
to package cars outside their old large home. Then, he
admired their hustle. Now he understood they had no
choice.

"When you talk to people at call centers, you can
tell they're not supposed to chat," Margo said. "They
must receive points for getting callers off the line. Then
they end the call by asking, 'Have I provided excellent
service today?'"

"Anybody who actually did provide excellent service would be fired," Tom said.

Margo knew she had more than once, when rid-
ing high in life, berated a clerk or laborer or other
person in a low-paid, no-future job. "Call centers and
eight-hundred numbers are maddening but we are
just reaping what we sowed," Margo said. "We were
the ones who demanded that everything be cheap
and fast."

"Last week I received a warning letter from the
district manager," Tom said.

Margo made the smallest cringe, then hated herself
for doing so. Tom hadn't told her this, which obviously
meant they had reached such straits that a letter from

some petty tyrant district manager at a delivery contractor had upset Tom.

"I was on a route, old lady answers the door when
I ring to leave her box. Tells me someone has broken
into her house. Of course it's her imagination. But
she lives alone. To comfort her I go in, walk around
the house with her, show her no one is there. Open
all the closets with her. District manager wants to
know why the computer log of when I scanned the
package bar code to when the truck moved again shows
I was parked in front of the same house for eight
minutes, eighteen seconds. Time is money, says he.
Docked me an hour's pay."

"Doing an old lady a favor for eight minutes, and
they docked you an hour?"

"Time is money, says he."

"All this rushing, isn't there a government regula-
tion or something?"

"You just said it. Our generation—we demanded
lower prices, everything fast and at discount. Wasn't
government's idea, was our idea. For twenty dollars,
FedEx takes a package cross-country in two days,
brings it to your door, rings the bell. For thirty-five dollars, cross-country overnight. And still the customers
complain it's not cheap enough."

Low-priced products are made possible by replacing workers with machines, after doing a cost-benefit analysis. If a worker earns $50,000 a year in pay and benefits, and she can be replaced with a capital investment that costs $250,000 after the tax breaks, then the machine will pay itself back in five years. Plus machines might need repair but never get sick; ones that fail are junked. People get sick and require long-term care, then pensions.

If a machine's payback period is five years, that's a precarious call for management, since in five years the machine may be obsolete, in which case you were better off staying with the worker. But if the prices of capital equipment for automation fall, and say the payback comes in two years, definitely replace the person with the machine. Prices for automation equipment were falling—partly because machines were beginning to build machines.

As for services, making prices keep falling in inflation-adjusted terms is possible only by running from the curb, by canceling employee benefits, by paying people for eight hours when they work ten, by laying personnel off at the slightest downturn then imposing mandatory overtime when business is good.

Delivering packages all day—most of them ordered from warehouse-based companies that offered good prices by cutting labor and health-care costs—Tom knew this too well. "Our generation, we were the ones who realized we could go to a store and get an hour of a salesman's time explaining product options, then go home, put the product ID number into Google and order over the Internet for less," he said. "We thought we were sticking it to the man. We were sticking it to the man's employees."

"At least delivery is physical. Can't be outsourced to Cambodia," Margo said.

Tom shook his head. Some trends such as declining factory employment were inevitable. After all, if improved technology had been outlawed in the 1950s, we'd be driving 8 mpg cars with no seat belts. But did that mean every economic trend should be accepted as inevitable?

"The cardiologists and bankers, the real-estate brokers and management consultants—they love outsourcing because it's good for corporate dividends and it drives down prices where they shop," Tom said. "Outsourcing hasn't come for them yet. Wait till high-paying white-collar jobs start being done remotely via broadband from the opposite hemisphere. Then the people with the cushy insider positions will scream bloody murder."

Margo said, "When we were set in life, we believed in a better world. But what did we do to create one?" She let the thought hang. Practically everyone of Margo and Tom's generation said they believed in a better world. What specific thing did any of them do to bring one about?

Tom knew that even he, as a goodhearted man, had spent more of his life indulging minor complaints than working toward the better tomorrow he would have told a pollster he favored. Tom once sat in his expansive corner office and stewed if someone important hadn't paid attention when he was speaking at a meeting. Felt ill-used if he didn't win an award that should have been his due. If the family vacation cabin wasn't close enough to the lakefront. If all the parking spaces were gone when he arrived. If the forks weren't chilled.

"Now that my eyes are open, I feel ashamed of how spoiled I was," Tom said. He'd been sitting for a while yet his breathing still was a bit irregular.

"There is nothing wrong with being spoiled. The only thing wrong is that everybody isn't spoiled."

Tom looked up as though he had something terrible to relate: "Today I delivered a package to Gresham Cooper. Remember him?"

"Of course! We had brunch with him and Melanie at the Ritz-Carlton." Margo tried to laugh at her own words, adding, "That was, ah, some while back."

"I get a package addressed to him. Marked Fragile—a set of Williams-Sonoma sommelier glasses. His new place is in the Cresthaven Woods development. Very nice, $1.6 mil for the entry models, comes with membership in their pool and tennis club. I was praying nobody would be home, but he answered the bell."

"That must have been awkward."

"When he recognized me, he thought it was some prank. You know, I dressed up as a delivery guy in order to play a joke."

"Did you play along?"

"I blurted it out—repeatedly laid off, desperate for money. He didn't know what to say. I could see he was trying to figure out whether he should tip me."

"Did he?" Margo's question was not entirely idle.

"Sure didn't invite me in to talk. Standing at the door I was looking past him into his house. Blond wood, Noguchi tables, wine racks, grand piano. Taste-less modern art—the surest sign you've made it in life. Serene and prosperous. I wanted to go in so badly."

"Luck will change for us, Tom."

"That kind of house stands for how our generation lost its way. Yet I want so badly to be in it. I want so badly to open the door and see you and the girls inside."

"There is nothing wrong with wanting to live in a beautiful house," Margo said.

"You should be in a house like that. You will be. It's what I owe you. But I will never enter that house again."

"Tom, our luck will change." She meant to placate him and hadn't understood what he said.

"You will live in a beautiful house again. The girls will come home from school and open the door to a place of plenty. It's all laid out."

Replaying in her head the tape of the conversation, Margo heard again what he said a moment before, and felt the vise of panic.

"Tom, what are you saying?"

"It's all laid out. You and the girls will live in a house in a place with a name like Cresthaven. You will never look at prices in restaurants. You will order from

Williams-Sonoma. But I will not experience these things again."

"Tom, you're scaring me! Are you going to break the law?"

"Not me, never. I am one of those suckers who plays by the rules."

The business leaders and politicians who will tell any lie for money or power, do they repent on their deathbeds? On their deathbeds they think, "I did what I wanted, I got what I wanted, I fucked who I wanted and I never paid any price. I was smart, not like those fools who play by the rules."

Whether a person can sin through life, then repent on his deathbed and win admission to glory, has been debated at least since Constantine, who followed exactly this formula. Tom suspected most who attain power or wealth don't bother to repent. Rather, they revel in the knowledge that they did whatever they wanted while people like Tom, held back by ethics, carried the weight of society.

Tom's voice was hollow and his tone approached self-pitying as he called himself a sucker—so unlike the gleaming young man she'd bumped into that day in Chicago. Margo did not know how to get him to talk about what was on his mind, or to explain the plan he had vaguely referred to over the past two years.

"I did it today," Tom said, plainly.

" 'It'?"

"Applied at McDonald's. I can work a full shift Saturday and a half shift Sunday. That's all I can stand. I must have a few hours a week when I'm not working. Assistant manager, $14.85 an hour. Minus uniform deduction."

"Tom, no! Things are not so bad that we need a third job in the family."

"The car insurance will be canceled if I don't bring in another hundred a week. We're paying on extended plan as it is and I'm still short. And I've got to cover that cash-advance loan somehow. The way they add interest, each week we owe more."

Once they'd had gold-plated credit, borrowing at just above prime. Now they were borrowing at 23 percent. Those whose situations are secure receive the best deals; those who are struggling get the short end, which holds them back from escaping from struggle.

McDonald's! In one of its locations Margo years ago complained, in a too-loud voice, as though she were visiting royalty, because one of the girls' Happy Meals contained a boy's toy rather than the requested girl's toy. Margo made a cross face at a minimum-wage worker who barely spoke English. The memory of this incident, which lasted perhaps all of ninety seconds, lent Margo discomfort. She might have caused the woman to be taken aside and yelled at by a superior. Even if not, she'd given a low-paid person in an inferior position a hard time about something inexpressibly minor.

Generally people are courteous to their social and financial equals. How you treat those who earn far less than you—it was not the fashion to say "beneath you," but class relationships continue regardless of fashion—is one of the tests of character. The politician or corporate boss or school principal or football coach who screams at interns or secretaries or sophomores is a person of low character. The incident had been years ago, but Margo felt no small discomfort at the memory of castigating a fast-food worker.

McDonald's! Was it everything wrong with America, or everything right? The company's cheeseburgers are good, and the world was voting with its feet on this point. People benefit from inexpensive cheeseburgers, especially average people who can't afford sit-down dining. Nobody puts a gun to anyone's head and makes the person buy a Big Mac rather than spend the same amount on lentils and fresh vegetables. And wasn't McDonald's adding fruit and yogurt options?

Margo felt that to work in a McDonald's or any similar place as a teenager, or as a recently arrived immigrant learning to fit in, even as a retiree wanting a little extra cash for part-time hours, was impossible to argue with. But for adult breadwinners to be able to find no better employment than a fast-food counter was an indictment of society. She shivered to think of Tom standing by the register on Saturday night, urging customers to add fries to their orders.

"We'll move somewhere small and live simply," Margo said. "The country is caught up in gotta-have-it, gotta-get-it. Let's move to a small town. Leave the rat race, the traffic jams, the status preening. Watch Fourth of July fireworks from the high-school bleachers. We could be twice as happy with half as much."

They'd just moved as it was, so Tom knew they could not afford to move again now—maybe in a year. Tom liked the idea of the simple life in a small town, but had looked at the numbers. Assuming they rented a truck and did all the lifting themselves, moving would cost at least $2,000, plus more deposit money upfront to rent in the new location, plus a total gamble on finding jobs.

Why do a billion members of the world's underclass remain in slums and shantytowns? Because they can't afford to move. The same could apply, though in a much different way, to Americans caught in economic currents. When Detroit automakers began their first big retrenchment, in the late 1970s, a few who lost jobs pulled up stakes and moved to growth areas such as Texas or Arizona. There they were known as "black taggers," for the simple white-on-black Michigan license plate of the period. Most who got out may have been glad they did. But many couldn't afford to move.

And another move would cause the girls to think they had become vagrants. Tom and Margo had engaged in elaborate pretenses to shelter the girls from the family's economic reality. Obviously their daughters sensed something amiss; perhaps they knew everything—children always know more about what's going on than their parents think. But Caroline and Megan did not press for details—what's happening with the family and money is such a scary topic. If they moved yet again, there could be no more pretending.

"I was in Bank of America yesterday—"

"Where before we were VIP Platinum," Margo interjected. She was amused by the contemporary usage of the word "platinum" to mean "exceptionally special," considering ninety-nine of a hundred people had never encountered the metal and wouldn't know it if some were placed in their laps.

"They couldn't have cared less what we used to be. I tried to talk to the bank about restructuring what we owe, to move the payday-loan debt into regular financing. They said we're now a bad risk. They were sharp. Laser focus on their own bottom line, plus tax-payer subsidies. Nice work if you can get it."

His expression became drained, though not for lack of thought. "I was pulling big bucks, I'd met the governor and knew members of Congress, I could have spoken out against the inequity of life and didn't," he said. "I feel in some way I deserve this fate. Promise me you will be sure the girls do not repeat my mistake."

Margo assumed that by "fate" he meant their financial circumstances.

She could not stand to hear him forlorn. "Tom, don't speak of yourself like that," she said, touching his hand. "You are a good man. If only every man was like you! You are what God hoped for when He made the world."

Tom looked at her as if grateful for the courtesy of a compliment he did not deserve; Margo was not the sort of person to invoke the divine. Then something caused him to decide to tell her.

"I kept up the payments on the executive life insurance policy," he said, as if to reveal that he had kept up payment were to reveal a shameful secret. "It's one of the reasons we are always desperate for cash. The premium is a thousand dollars a month. I've paid it."

"Tom, why? We need that money for other things!"

On any subject other than Tom, Margo's mind already would have snapped to the realization of *why*.

"Whenever I'm exhausted, whenever I despair, I console myself with the thought that no matter how many ways I have failed, I have kept up the premiums on that policy. You and the girls will have five million."

"You don't mean—"

"No, not that," he said. "Of course I would not kill myself." He smiled just a bit. "But the world may do it for me. I have a heart condition. It's bad. You remember that was what took my father. I've known about mine since a few months after we lost our health insurance. So I kept up the life policy."

Margo struggled to speak, feeling something beyond panic. She was angry at Tom for not confiding in her, angry at herself for not pressing him about his secret, angry at God for threatening to take Tom away. She had tried to visualize the divine, or to direct a thought toward the Maker, only a few times in her adult life. Now this had happened twice in a single minute.

"Self-pay, the operation is forty thousand dollars," Tom began. He wanted her to know he had researched the situation, worked out the practicalities. "The hospital demands half as cash up front, plus my signature on a garnishee agreement that lasts till the balance is paid, including interest and penalties. But if I have a bad enough heart attack and arrive at an emergency room near death, then they operate regardless of ability to pay. The Obama legislation might change this, but not till the year 2014. That may be too late for me."

"You can't mean—" Her mind had raced to the end of a dark corridor of thought.

"That is exactly what I mean. The only way out is to force myself to have a heart attack. That's why I keep pushing myself. If my heart stops and I am gasping for air, then they will save me. Not because they care. Because they fear the liability."

Margo, a strong and independent woman, began to sob like a frightened child. She could not find any consoling thought, imagine anything positive to say. Margo wanted to be a little girl again, safe in her bed, calling for her mother to bring her a glass of water. She collapsed into Tom's arms and wept.

"You don't have to worry about this," Tom said.

Rather than seem frightened or troubled, Tom was resolute. He smiled, showing the calm demeanor of the man who has accepted fate and in so doing, been released from fear.

In that moment, Tom appeared again to Margo as he had when she first saw him on the street in Chicago—a handsome, lean young man of unlimited promise, a catch any girl would want. In that moment Tom knew again the engaging voice and smooth confidence of his youth. He was granted a moment of showing again all the qualities that made him the love of Margo's life, as if they were starting fresh, not approaching the end.

"It's all laid out, one way or the other," Tom said. "I am likely to have a heart attack. If I do, and the ambulance comes, they'll fix me and we will be together for a long time. If the ambulance doesn't come, then you and the girls are set for life financially. It's all laid out. I vowed to take care of you, and I will."

Margo was limp, sobbing. Tom knew this was the moment to broach with her the hardest part.

"I've been through every scenario. If chest pains start I can't go right to the hospital. That way they could stabilize me and turn me out. I've got to wait until it's a full heart attack—so they operate." He said these things confidently and brightly, as if describing a big promotion he'd just won or a luxury vacation in the planning.

Normally Margo would understand instantly where Tom was going, but she was sobbing and could not think. He realized he had to spell this out, and so continued: "If we're together when the moment comes, you must promise not to call 911 right away. I've got to arrive in bad shape. That way, either I get the operation free and am fine, or it's too late and you receive the money. If you call 911 immediately and they stabilize me, the nightmare just starts all over."

Tom paused. "Promise me if I start showing the signs of heart failure, you will wait five minutes before calling 911." He said this as plainly as if he were saying, "Promise me you'll be at the restaurant at eight."

"No! No! No!"

"No!" was the only word Margo could choke out. She pounded on his chest, source of this sudden horror, crying No, no, no, no.

Tom was calm, having reconciled himself to what would come. "This could end with me fine," he said in his voice of youthful potential. "If it ends with me gone, the girls' future will be secured. As they grow, the girls will know their father acted in their best interest. They will love me and honor my memory."

Margo was a marionette with the strings severed. She couldn't control her limbs or make her mouth move properly. She pressed against him, trembling, saying over and over again—No, no, no.

"I have steeled myself," Tom said. "If I am given the chance to choose, I will choose to do right by you and our daughters."

She continued to sob, unable to construct words. All her life, Margo had charged directly toward problems. This turn of events terrified her so deeply she simply went limp.

Tom held her, stroked her hair and looked on her with deep longing. After a while, Tom carried Margo to the master bed and lay with her, embracing. Though it was early, she fell into shattered sleep. Tom thought if she could rest awhile, when the girls got home, they would take her mind off things. He covered Margo with a blanket and kissed her forehead, whispering into her ear his love for her.

Then Tom slipped off the bed and went down to the kitchen, looking for the dinner he'd missed. He opened a beer, made a sandwich and had taken the first bite when he knew a strange sensation, as if he could feel the inside of his body. Maybe carrying his wife to the bedroom had not been history's greatest idea.

The sensation passed. Tom felt normal again, and thought he might go out for a walk. The area around the building was set up for cars, not for walking: even so, getting some air is always good. When Tom tried to stand to go outside, he needed to brace himself against the kitchen table.

The pain got worse a lot faster than Tom expected. He put the phone into his hand but did not dial. Tom knew he had to be strong and not cry out, since Margo would dial 911 immediately if she woke.

The pain became awful. Tom thought, *Why does it have to happen now, when I haven't said good-bye to the girls?* Then he thought, *I can take this. I have to take this. They'll understand. They'll know this was my duty. They'll be back in a beautiful house and I will be able to see them.*

Tom wondered how long was long enough before

dialing 911. His breath was sporadic—had he already waited long enough? He decided to wait ten more seconds before dialing 911, and began to count aloud, "One-thousand one, one-thousand two, one-thousand three, one-thousand four . . ." He heard a voice calling his name, as if from far away. The voice was pleasant, reassuring. Someone was calling to him.

Chapter 10

October 2010

Dow Jones Index returns to the level of 2001.
Nobel Prize in Economics awarded for
analysis of "frictional unemployment."
Google speeds searches to half a second,
promising this will save one day of a typical
person's life.

The new place was splendid, though lacking the quirky character of the house she and Tom lost to foreclosure. Recently built homes tend to feel as if designed by machines. Many are branded with model names—the Windsor, the Craftsman Manor, the Apex Grande, the Shana Vista. Customers seeking a new home are supposed to ask for branded models, saying to builders, "I want a Foxwoods Supreme." If you liked the Foxwoods Supreme look in the front but the Napa Sunset layout in the back, a computer could generate that from software. Having the computer customize your house was said by the sales office to give it a human touch.

The bells and whistles on the new place, Margo had to admit, were entertaining. When someone left a bathroom, the lights turned themselves off; if someone stepped in, the lights turned themselves on. The dishwasher was hidden in the kitchen island, the toaster and coffeemaker recessed behind a panel. The furnaces monitored their filters. When a filter needed to be changed, the furnace-control chip used the Internet to order a replacement, which arrived from Amazon in two days.

The countertops were "engineered quartz"—even more expensive than Roman granite. Seeming to hang without support on a wall, the very thin HD LCD TV could be pulled out, swiveled, then pushed back flush when not in use. All wireless equipment was inside a disguised closet so as not to be unsightly, and there was space for expansion—for electronic devices not yet invented. The master bedroom, with a clear view of the eastern sky, had a broad window with an optical screen that would descend on servos, so those in the California-king-sized master bed could watch the sunrise without their eyes being dazzled. To close the deal, the builder threw in a grand piano for the living room, a touch Margo had always wanted in a home.

The girls viewed the technology of the new house as the order of things—of course the furnace talks to the Internet.

For the past year Caroline and Megan had their own rooms again, a status address again, a great school again—one of *Newsweek*'s top-rated public schools. Caroline, a junior, had already made friends in one of the positive-influence peer groups, was on varsity field hockey, got cast as Bloody Mary in *South Pacific*, was taking the Advanced Placement course in government studies. Megan, a freshman, was on the JV basketball team, a fledgling reporter for the school newspaper and in honors in her core courses. She was tracking toward Advanced Placement as a junior, maybe even an AP course as a sophomore. The girls had changed in manifold ways from the period when they seemed headed for juvenile delinquency. Money does not buy happiness, but sure can fix problems.

The sign at the entrance to the development, a sign lighted and bordered with gold-painted filigree, read SUMMIT HAVEN WOODS. The sign felt to Margo as if it glowed with approval when owners of houses in the development returned home.

By the sign were saplings that had been planted during construction of the development. There were no "woods" anywhere in sight, just the saplings and ornamental shrubs. Old neighborhoods draw their character partly from trees: in modern high-efficiency construction, land first is leveled, then houses built, then trees replanted. Doing it that way speeds construction and lowers cost, though results in impressive new homes that appear planted in a fallow field.

By the time saplings were grown into mature trees, the girls would be adults with children of their own, and that would be the sign to leave this place. Then this house would be sold, and the next family to move in would observe the old, full trees and think of Summit Haven Woods as a long-established neighborhood in an arboretum. The spirits of those here first would have dissipated from the place and would mean nothing to those who came next.

Already Margo could see herself twenty years in the future, gazing wistfully on the mature trees and reminiscing about her daughters' youth. She knew she had but to snap her fingers and "Pomp and Circumstance" would be playing at their college graduations. She'd snap her fingers again and see an old woman, asking the mirror, "So soon?"

Margo and Lillian were having wine in the living room, near the piano. Margo was in the early stages of lessons, determined to learn to play.

Initially Margo thought she shouldn't try piano with the girls around because their boyfriends would hear her practice errors over the cell phones. Nothing embarrasses teens more than parents attempting to act young, and learning instruments is supposed to be done during one's school years.

Then Caroline explained to her mother that teens rarely speak on the phone, only text. When cell devices became common, companies that sold them assumed people would yak, yak, yak: pricing focused on the minutes, with texting as a throw-in. Teens and college kids rapidly realized texting is more efficient than talking. No need for salutations and chitchat, no awkward pauses or questions about tone, just the info. Plus every text was like receiving a letter, if a very succinct, coded letter of low import. Everyone likes to open the mailbox and find letters.

The women had been conversing about events in France, where, the previous day, nearly a million people rioted over a government plan to raise the national retirement threshold to the shocking age of sixty-two. France is easy to make fun of. But the French take six weeks' paid vacation annually, produce more GDP per capita than the Japanese while spending far less time on the job and live longer than Americans. Is their approach to social organization really so off-base?

The conversation shifted to a faculty event Lillian had attended: "So then I caused this huge flap at the dinner for the department heads. I accidentally insulted a leading postmodernist."

"How?"

"I called one of his theories 'true.'"

Margo felt pleased that she stayed in enough touch with the intellectual world that she got the joke. At least Lillian had not accused an academic of a really serious offense, like believing in something. Margo felt equally good that she had her own reference to the subject.

"The other day I ate in this chic place downtown that bills itself a 'postmodern restaurant,'" she said. "Expensive, snobby, strange dishes. 'Postmodern' was the right word. None of the food could be said with assurance to taste either good or bad."

"Was it the kind of place where they grill cotton candy with heritage kale and free-range bison?"

"Yes."

Lillian said, "Oh, I love restaurants like that! They

certainly keep one from overeating. At the height of the Asian-French fusion fad, I thought every possible combination of ingredients had already been used by celebrity chefs. Now I realize that was close-the-patent-office thinking. There will never be an end to ridiculous dishes, so long as people are willing to pay too much."

"I'll give you the name of this place," Margo said. "It's very hard to get in. When you phone for a reservation, you get an answering machine that says in a foreign accent, 'How dare you call us!'"

"Brilliant marketing."

"Tom says he won't eat anywhere that does not advertise steak and whiskey."

"In twenty years, it will be illegal to advertise steak and whiskey. Probably already is in California."

The house was too quiet, because the girls had gone to a sleepover: gone together happily, without hysterics or pouting, another recent uptick in their behavior. The new house, with its sense of steady affluence, was the psychotropic they needed.

In the quiet, Margo heard some mechanism click on and whir. The new home included an extra refrigerator in the garage, for the overflow of suburban living—beer, Gatorade, diet soda. Margo kept a selection of Carvel ice-cream cakes on standby in the garage freezer, in case teens dropped by unexpectedly.

The extra refrigerator, the builder explained, is a specially engineered garage unit. Because a garage gets cold in winter, the cooling elements in a regular fridge shut down, allowing the contents to warm even as it is cold around the box. Solution? The garage refrigerator has a heated cooling element. When it's cold, one part of the machine makes heat in order to warm another part that makes cold. Thus a device drawing energy from the burning of fossil fuels keeps things artificially cold when it's already naturally cold. Isn't this a great country!

Margo told Lillian, "Megan removed the stud from her tongue. She went through our photo albums, taking away any picture where you could see it."

"Save one to blackmail her with when she's older."

"When we were young, in order to gross out our parents the boys wore long hair and the girls refused to wear dresses," Margo said. "Today's kids pierce their eyebrows in order to gross out their parents. Once today's kids have children, what will be left for their kids to do in order to gross them out?"

"Perhaps they'll shave their heads and tattoo things onto their skulls."

"Please don't suggest that around Caroline's boy-friend," Margo said quickly.

With satisfaction, Margo changed to a topic she could not talk about too much: "I'm already thinking ahead to Caroline's college visits over spring break. Her first choice is Cornell—that's pretty ambitious, need-less to say. But the college counselor thinks she has a chance at a top school. Caroline's done an admissions-essay draft, about what she learned when her father was a delivery driver and her mom worked at Hooters."

Mention of her final waitressing job made Margo chuckle.

"I'm glad you can laugh about that now," Lillian said.

"At least they wanted me! Anyway, the college counselor thinks her essay will be a hit."

"Brace yourself about the visits. Spring break is Mercedes gridlock at any top college campus."

"I'm the last person to begrudge a mom her driv-ing a child to college in a fancy car," Margo said. "But half of the people in the Mercedes demographic spend their office hours awarding themselves bonuses while cutting benefits for single parents. Tom says the mod-ern CEO considers a corporate jet for himself more important than a living wage for his workers."

Above the fireplace was a magnificent portrait of Tom as a young man: walking along a beach against a stiff wind, squinting off into a sunset. The picture was taken by a friend of Margo's who was an amateur photographer—taken sufficiently long ago that the camera used was the kind that had film inside.

The three of them had gone to the beach at the foot of East Division Street to take a photo of Tom and Margo for their engagement announcement. The day wore on, the wind kicked up. After they were finished and preparing to leave, the photographer turned for a "grab" shot of Tom—a picture the subject does not expect to be taken. Margo loved the image, which was not just a good photograph of her husband but a good photograph, period. And she loved that he was staring in contemplation at the same lake she had contemplated as a child.

"But what can we do about it?" Lillian asked, on the topic of luxury at the top. "Back in the age of the robber baron there were only a few of the disgustingly rich; they were rare and easy to hate. Now there are entire zip codes of people who have more money than they need, and they keep getting better off while the rest of the country stagnates. Those at the top are just playing the angles of the system—who can blame them? Until the system is reformed, they'll keep raking it in. Anyway, there are far too many of them to hate."

The American economy had become like a casino where a small number of people start with most of the chips, then laud themselves for winning. Granted a second chance at affluence, Margo wanted to make a difference. She'd read an essay that said it is unrealistic to expect an individual to change the world, but all are obligated to try to change what is directly around them. That made sense. So Margo had signed up with a group of young activists who were starting an advocacy campaign for a county-level living-wage statute.

Tom said charity and government programs were well and good but what average people needed was money, then they could decide for themselves how to use it. That a person could work a forty-hour week in the United States and still be impoverished by the federal definition—that just wasn't right. Higher wages, not more government giveaways, were the solution.

Margo couldn't be sure her involvement with a poorly organized advocacy group would accomplish anything beyond making her feel better about herself. So far she'd mainly had a lot of twentysomethings over and fed them dinner while they discussed extremely grand plans. As the voice of maturity, she told them to demand the sun, moon and sky and settle for whatever they could get. Regardless, she was done with sitting around complaining about why others fail to act.

"What I don't understand," Margo said, to Lillian's point, "is why the people with a lot of money don't give it away in order to have fun."

The amounts the well-off lavish on themselves, if spent in Africa, would save human lives in large numbers. One would think the greatest satisfaction attainable on Earth would be the saving of lives. One would think this would motivate the wealthy to give money away not to achieve a better world—a better world would be the bonus—but rather to make themselves feel good. That is to say, the rich should give their money away for selfish reasons.

"Some hand over a small fraction of their net worth in order to achieve social acclaim, that's all," Lillian said.

"Yet by hoarding money they harm themselves, missing their own chance to experience joy. I mean, who is the happiest character in all of literature? Scrooge, because becoming generous allows him to achieve a feeling akin to bliss. Why don't people with a lot of money realize that generosity would be more fun than anything they could purchase?"

"It wasn't so much that Scrooge became generous," Lillian countered. "What happened is that he became aware of the humanity of those around him. Most of the very well off can't conceptualize this. They believe they were chosen for wealth, and others chosen to struggle—that the whole notion of egalitarianism goes against the order of things. It's a three-thousand-year-old Hindu concept but Christianity has done its share of promoting this bullshit too." Lillian rarely used strong language.

The same economic and technological forces causing living standards to rise across most of the globe also were causing wealth to concentrate at the top. The bitter comes with the sweet: rising living standards are sweet, so perhaps some wealth concentration is unobjectionable. But if markets remained free and borders remained open, inevitably the top few percent would keep accelerating away from the rest. The social system was making those at the top wealthy—why shouldn't they show gratitude by returning more of what they possessed as taxes and philanthropy? Surely the rich are better off in circumstances of high income plus taxation than they would be without income or taxation.

A small number at the top give freely, being admirable individuals. Most of the wealthy keep everything for themselves, because most people are self-centered—that's human nature. Since most at the top always will horde, fundamental reform of the system is needed. Counting on altruism is like praying for rain.

The conversation turned to the girls. Many contemporary parents talk compulsively of their children. The childless can find this oppressive, and not just because one can stand only so much discussion of how clever, gifted and precocious someone else's offspring are. Contemporary parents are especially wrapped up in their children's test scores and grades, as if the parents themselves were being graded. But Lillian saw what Margo's girls had been through and considered constant discussion of them inevitable.

Megan's arrival at high school, Margo told her friend, had occasioned another iteration of the Big Talk—this time as the Really Big Talk. Today many girls get the Big Talk Lite in middle school, when it's phrased as a hypothetical, followed by the Really Big Talk in freshman year. Margo started to joke about what the boys' version might be like but then bit her tongue, knowing Lillian would never have these conversations with any child of her own.

Lillian shook her head and said, "To think I spent all those years elaborately trying to avoid pregnancy, having unpleasant arguments with dates and boyfriends, only to find out later that I never could anyway. I might have been a carefree sex addict, and didn't know that till too late. God has a sense a humor. But it's slapstick humor."

As far as Margo could tell, Lillian truly did not care about not having married. But the death of her young daughter was something she had never really recovered from, and perhaps never would. Leading the conversation in that direction had been clumsy on Margo's part.

"I'm sorry, I didn't mean to make you think about—"

"It's all right," Lillian said. "Every day something happens that makes me think of Madeline."

"I haven't heard you speak her name in years."

"I am trying to get more comfortable with using her name," Lillian said. Like many who live alone, she could be preoccupied with various forms of self-monitoring.

Margo didn't know what to say. On some topics,

there is nothing that sounds right. Needing to sustain the conversation, Margo said what she usually did not. "Things must happen for a reason."

"I find consolation in the assumption that things do not happen for a reason," Lillian replied. "It's all chance and circumstances. Life is a random fall down the staircase. The tragedies of history would be inexplicable if things happened for a reason."

"That's a depressing thought."

"It is a life-affirming thought," Lillian said, with some force.

They had touched on a subject to which she had devoted considerable contemplation. "A car crash kills a teenager, that happened to fulfill God's plan? Plan for what, for that teenager? For that road? For the insurance company? An earthquake kills thousands, that happened because of divine will? People die of diseases caused by mindless organisms, the germ proteins were under the control of supernatural agency? A child falls into water and drowns, that happened *for a reason?*"

As a refined woman, Lillian liked to attribute the notions she espoused to others—to some writer, researcher or newspaper columnist. It's safer to attribute to others.

But these thoughts came from her heart and were keenly felt. She continued, "Now, if the earthquake happened because there was a flaw in the Earth's crust, if the disease was caused by some failure of cell structure—then events become comprehensible. If the child fell into the water because the nanny wasn't watching or because there was no guardrail, the death is still awful, but comprehensible. To say that most calamities are accidents devoid of significance is the positive view. I could not get up in the morning and face the day unless I believed most tragedies are completely arbitrary."

Margo knew these statements were deft as a matter of logic, but thought her friend was not considering emotion. "Believing everything happens for a reason can relieve you of torment," Margo said. "You can imagine there is some larger purpose behind events."

"I should rather sob forever than think a child died because a higher power desired her death. There is less sorrow if there is no larger purpose! If I thought my daughter's death happened for a purpose, I would be inconsolable."

"I don't mean specific people are chosen to die at specific points; that's very hard to believe. I mean—we cannot know what chain of events will be caused. Sometimes bad leads to good."

"One of the nurses actually told me Madeline died to show me my life was worth living," Lillian said. She teared up. "That Madeline was born, suffered and died to teach a lesson to me."

"No one knows what to say to someone who has just lost a loved one," Margo said. "People become nervous and make dumb remarks. We've both been through it. You shouldn't take such comments seriously."

"The nurse who said that wasn't just using some figure of speech, she meant it," Lillian replied. "Said Madeline died because everything happens for a reason."

"She thought saying that would give you comfort."

"All the love I gave Madeline, the distance I traveled to find her, the obstacles to adopting her, the hours I spent at her side when she got sick—I would go mad if I thought what happened was anything other than a random, numbing malfunction of biochemistry."

Everything happens for a reason. Many believe God controls events, sees the future: that all that occurs, wonderful or appalling, is the unfolding of an omnipotent plan. This view comes from clergy, hymnals and revival tents—not scripture. Far from depicting the Maker as controlling the world, the Bible depicts God as constantly surprised, upset, angry and frustrated by inability to bring about desired ends. Pretty much from the Garden of Eden forward, things don't go as expected: divine fury results. Eventually the Maker achieved serenity, expressed regret for the floods and atrocities—God has a shameful past—and said through the prophet Jeremiah, "I repent me of the evil I have done to you," meaning done to humanity.

One doesn't hear that verse oft-quoted in churches. People assume terrible things happen owing to divine will, that earthquakes are punishment for wayward nations and diseases retribution for sins. People assume this because they've listened to red-faced evangelists shouting about omnipotent control—which is the sort of claim that makes audiences give money to evangelists. Scripture elaborately documents the absence of omnipotence.

If the divine found serenity, perhaps someday human society will too. Then Maker and made can be reunited, and innocence regained by both. In its way, Lillian's view that most tragedies are accidents was a step in the direction of God.

"I think you should speak about Madeline more often," Margo said. "It's healthy. I say Tom's name constantly. I tell myself not to but can't stop."

"He would have liked this house," Lillian said.

Margo watched the fire dance. The house had a gas-powered fireplace run by wireless remote; flames rose from faux logs never consumed. Margo had wanted a regular fireplace in which to burn wood. The builder considered the request eccentric, practically risqué: didn't she care about convenience? The county council, she was told, banned new construction of real-wood fireplaces, owing to claims regarding second-hand smoke drifting down the street. Margo knew the day was coming when, seeking a sensual indulgence practical in age, she would have the air-conditioning and the fireplace on simultaneously.

"You've never really told me," Lillian said, not needing to add, *what happened that night.*

Lillian had walked toward the question of the specifics of Tom's passing many times and always, seeing pain on Margo's face, walked back. But now she had just talked about Madeline, her most painful subject. Perhaps this time Margo would talk about hers.

"The girls don't know the details, only that he had a heart attack and there was life insurance," Margo said. She was choosing words deliberately, but not addressing the issue just raised. "Should I ever tell them the full story? Maybe. Someday, if I am sure their lives are going well, the time will come for them to learn what their father gave up in their names. Maybe. I don't want to think about that question for many years."

Of course Margo knew she had not told her best friend much more than she'd told her daughters. This was not from lack of trust. But the full story seemed a private thing between her and her husband. That only she and Tom knew made it seem that Tom remained a presence, as the other half of a secret shared between them. If Margo told the secret to someone else, it would no longer be hers and Tom's solely.

As they sat watching the fake fire, Margo realized that should something take her, too, away—any person might be hit by a bus on a bright sunny day—all knowledge of that night would die with her.

Comprehension of this made Margo decide to tell her friend the entire account. Lillian sat in silence as she listened, not interjecting "Really?" or "And then what happened?" Margo just talked. Lillian stopped the story once, to ask why they hadn't come to her for money: she could have borrowed against her retirement savings. Margo explained that she did not find out how bad the situation really was until the last moment.

Near the end of the recounting Margo said, "I was lying in semi-sleep on the bed and I heard Tom saying that he loved me. I felt a kind of perfection of love, of a force that existed before we met and would continue long after we last glimpsed each other.

"I drifted off to sleep and don't know if a minute passed or an hour. You know how going to sleep can seem to be safety, then when you wake up, all your problems are still there. I thought I heard someone calling Tom's name from far away, in a kind voice. I must have been dreaming at that point. Things can seem real in a dream. The voice calling Tom seemed real.

"Then I heard a crash in the kitchen, a sound that was jarring and strange. I woke up, found him lying collapsed, the phone near his hand. I called 911, then pounded on his chest and blew into his mouth.

"It was our last kiss. I can still taste his spit—I hope I always will be able to. By the time the paramedics arrived, his soul had departed from his body."

There wasn't much Lillian could say. She asked, "You think there is a soul?"

"Maybe car crashes are chance," Margo said. "But

we cannot be here just to carry out coincidences involving molecular heat exchange. I see the generations of our day as some kind of stepping stone on a path toward a life without anxiety or harm. My children can live in a gentler world—or someone's children can."

Lillian said, "Supposing there can be a gentler world, it will not happen till long after you and I and everyone we know are gone."

"At least we've made a start."

The way men and women of the present look back on the Dark Ages—as a time of suffering, ignorance and abbreviated lives—is how men and women of the future may look back on the present. Perhaps our descendants won't be able to fathom how we were able to bear such short existences, under such stress, with so much belligerence, solitude and fixation on materialism. But at least we've made a start.

They sat without speaking for quite a while. Then Lillian looked down at her watch and noted, "Doesn't it always seem late?"

They agreed to meet again soon. Lillian said good night, and departed.

Margo was alone in the new house. She walked slowly from room to room, wishing the girls already were back. Whatever else she and Tom had or hadn't accomplished, they had raised the kind of children the world needed—informed, set free from the prejudices of the past. There are many children like that today, which gives hope.

Although alone, Margo spoke aloud, as if she could be heard: "Can you see us, Tom? We're in such a beautiful house. The bills are covered. I don't look at prices in restaurants, just like before. When Megan got her A in algebra, she asked for something Tiffany and it was no problem. I bought a Lexus, cash, no monthly payment. Deep Sea Mica. I didn't want the gold badges but the dealer threw them in."

Margo went onto the deck and gazed at the infinite sky. When pondering life the ancients looked upward, assuming up was the direction of origin. Now science shows that the firmament is far too large for Earth to be more than an asterisk, that "up" is relative to frame of reference. As for origin, it may be centuries or millennia before people find that answer, if the answer ever can be found.

Margo understood that even on the clearest night one can perceive only the tiniest fraction of what exists. The knowledge that she was a grain of dust in comparison to a hundred billion galaxies did not make her feel small—rather, made her feel needed. Without awareness, the stars would have nothing to warm. Margo considered the magnitude of the heavens reassuring, evidence this can't all be some celestial mistake. The firmament has existed for fourteen billion years—and stars are still forming. Compared to people, creation is immensely old. Compared to itself, the universe glistens with the dew of morning: may exist for unfathomable spans of time, if not forever. Who can say what the cosmic enterprise may be?

So the big picture is good—but ours is the little picture.

Margo asked aloud, "Will it all fall to pieces, Tom? The way we live today took you, Tom, it took you away, and you will not be the last victim. Have we produced these wonderful children just in time for things to fall apart? If everything falls apart, we can't put the blame on distant corporations or politicians we don't like. We will be to blame, all of us, for the country is as we demanded it be."

Margo felt calm, resolute and lonely. The world could not be trusted, but Tom had kept every promise he made to her. She hoped she would always be able to taste their last kiss.

Acknowledgments

For the realization of this book, thanks are due to my friends, colleagues and editors Jonathan Alter, Timothy Bartlett, Ethan Bassoff, James Bennet, Anne Bensson, Molly Bedell, Harold Boughton, David Brooks, Patricia Burke, Robin Campbell, Carolyn Carlson, Stephen Carter, Diane Chandler, Ta-Nehisi Coates, Masie Cochrane, Stephen Colbert, James Collins, Katharine DeShaw, Eric Dezenhall, Benedict Drew, Martha Drullard, Thomas Dunne, Mahidar Durbhakula, James Fallows, Donna Fenn, Henry Ferris, Sharon Fisher, Avra Friedfeld, Christ Gaetanos, Kathleen Gilligan, Janet St. Goar, Tedd Habberfield, Carla Hall, Laura Hall, Marjorie Hazen,

Katharine Herrup, Arianna Huffington, Debbie Ida, Jonathan Jao, Jan Jones, Mickey Kaus, Bob Kerrey, Michael Kinsley, Barbara Klie, Doro Koch, Robert Krimmer, William Lauerman, Emily Lazar, Alan Lelchuck, Nicholas Lemann, Jan Lewis, Ann Lindgren, Ben Loehnen, Deborah McGill, James Mallon, Rachelle Mandik, John Milner, Charles Peters, Sally Richardson, Janet Robinson, Tina Rosenberg, Claudia Russell, Charles Sciandra, Carolyn See, Kurt Schluntz, Mathew Shear, Allison Silver, Lauren Smythe, Kurt Snibbe, Barbara Snyder, Claire Swiat, Mary Thomas, Mary Ward, William Whitworth, David Wilson, Peter Wolverton and Claudia Zahn; to the memories of Fred Sondermann, 1923–1978; James Clay, 1927–1990; Christopher Georges, 1965–1998; John Robinson, 1953–2009; Samuel Starr, 1933–2011; William Goss, 1941–2011, and Jonathan Rowe, 1946–2011; to my children, Grant, Mara Rose and Spenser; to my siblings, Frank, Neil and Nancy; to my wife, Nan Kennelly.

I am indebted to Jonathan Karp, who a decade ago suggested I write a nonfiction book about the limits of economic knowledge, and call the volume *The Leading Indicators*. Somehow I was able to resist spending years interviewing economists. But the title stuck with me.